DRAGON'S SON

Book Three of the Ulfr Crisis

I0638362

BADELGARD, THE COUNTRY OF THE NORTHMEN

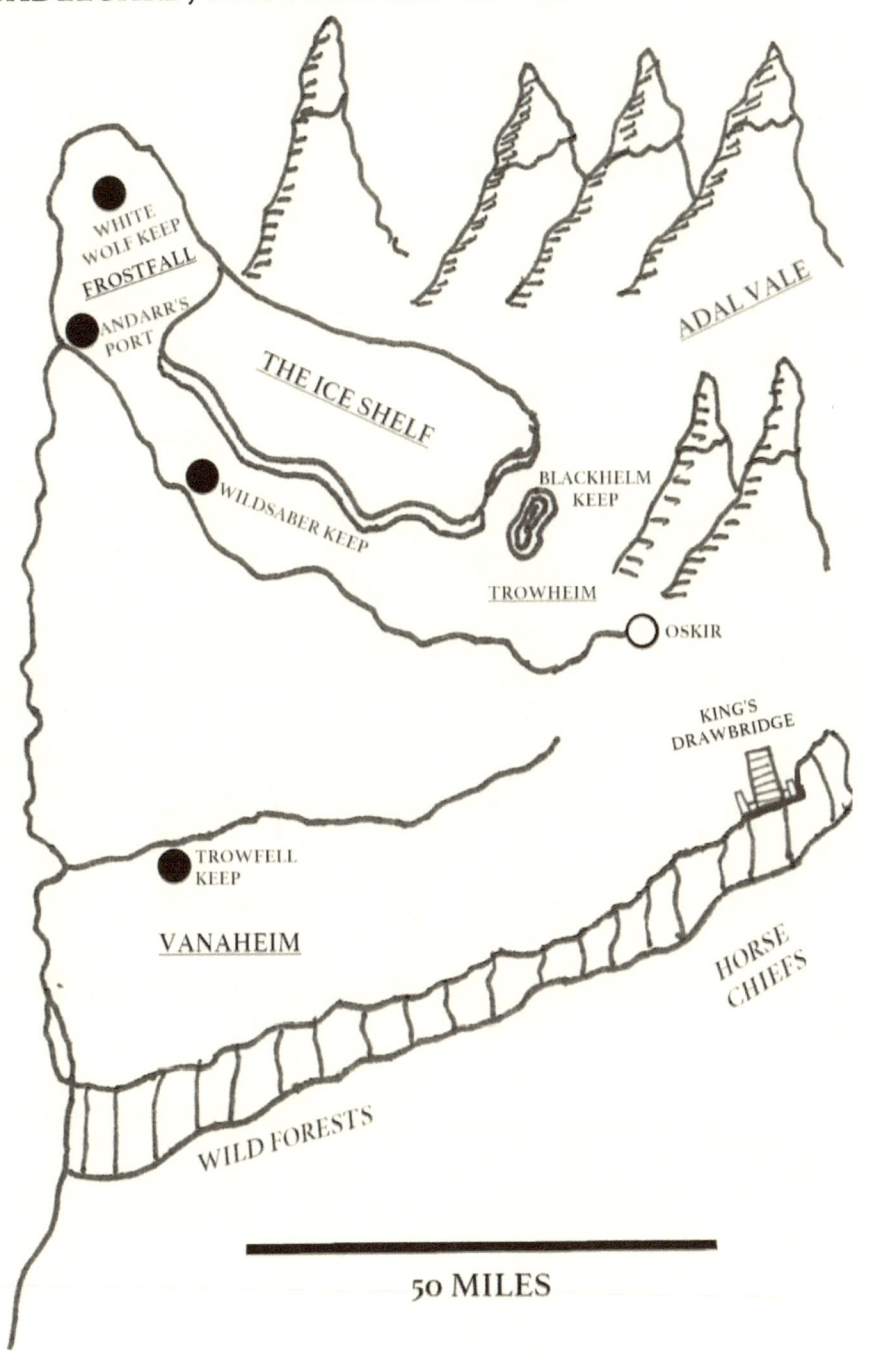

WHITE WOLF KEEP
FROSTFALL
ANDARR'S PORT

THE ICE SHELF

ADAL VALE

WILDSABER KEEP

BLACKHELM KEEP

TROWHEIM

OSKIR

KING'S DRAWBRIDGE

TROWFELL KEEP

VANAHEIM

HORSE CHIEFS

WILD FORESTS

50 MILES

Table of Contents

PART ONE:
MY BROTHER THE MORGUIS

CHAPTER ONE

Thorsten—or Huge Thorsten, as the small people of lowland Badelgard called him—had never seen anything like it. Nor had he, at any point in his life, thought he might. The Golden House, home of the High Kings of Badelgard, burning in a towering inferno. A column of smoke rose up high into the sky, easily visible from where Thorsten stood.

Perhaps it was even more disturbing from his vantage point: outside the door of the low-town inn. Now the lowborns, long poorly-treated, could see for themselves the unmaking of the king and his nobles. The outsiders—the foreigners who entered the city—had freed them from their shackles. But were they better off? Food was in scarce supply. The crops had, in all likelihood, failed. Soon starvation would set in.

Thorsten shivered at the thought.

The sight of the burning Golden House awakened in him something he had tried, in recent days, to suppress. For most of his adult life, Thorsten's lust of gold had ruled him. He had given no heed to the sanctity of life; he cared only about accumulating wealth, and the lives he had ended were without count.

But he had atoned. The goddess herself had come to him in a dream. He had thought himself beyond morality or compassion, beyond help… but one look in the eyes of the goddess, pure and holy, and the weight of his crimes fell upon his shoulders like a mountain. He had gone to Vanaheim, to the goddess's holy temple, and offered all the wealth he could to her—all the gold he had not spent on whores and mead. The goddess had forgiven him, but Thorsten knew someone who would not.

Thorsten's mother lived in Adal Vale. By all accounts, she was alive. Who knew how such a saint had given birth to such unfortunate twins—Gunstein and Thorsten, both thieves and murderers of the lowest degree. Was it her husband? That was anyone's guess. But

Thorsten's mother, though close in flesh, could not be further from Thorsten or Gunstein in spirit. Pious to the last, making offerings every week to the gods—at least, from what Thorsten remembered of his childhood. She would never accept him.

And yet, did he have a choice? Winter was coming, and it promised to be the harshest in history. Who knew what had happened to Gunstein? In all likelihood, he was dead: food for worms. And no one would know or sing of him; no one would care. Thorsten and Gunstein, after a falling-out over gold, had split up. And Thorsten could only envision death in his brother's future. It was the price one paid for the kind of life they led.

But regardless, Thorsten had to go to Adal Vale before starvation set in. The evil that had entered Badelgard would not climb so high into the upper mountains; it had not in ancient times, and it would not again. Even if starvation touched the lowland, the valemen were hunters, not farmers. And no matter how cold it grew, no matter how deep the chill, the hunter's bow could always find its mark. Venison and bear meat, trout and mutton from highland goats—those would remain. The greatest question for Thorsten, the one that meant everything to him, was whether his mother would forgive him for the way he led his life.

But he had to go. The burning of the Golden House—the bright flame and the column of dark-gray smoke—showed that the old Badelgard was coming to an end. He would have to go back to Adal Vale. Everything he had was gone; in the high mountain passes rested his only hope.

He had to go now.

He had to prepare for what would be a long journey. Market stalls, set up in the middle of low-town, offered the last scrapings of road-biscuits. The shopkeeper had long abandoned his post, in all likelihood due to the commotion at the Golden House. Thorsten took a handful—perhaps more than was warranted—and tossed it in his sack.

But as a gesture of his changed persona, he left the remainder of his money there on the desk: a dented silver penny, and two farthings. All that was left of his life of crime, wasted on years of whores and drunkenness.

A tear fell as he heaved the sack over his shoulders. Past the streets of low-town, beyond the frantic screaming that rose above the crackling flame, Huge Thorsten walked out of the Golden Gate and into the snowy lands beyond.

The wooden markers rose above the snow, showing the path to Huge Thorsten. The day was fading; the sun, pale and weak, grew ever lower in the sky. Thorsten felt the worm of unease wriggling in his stomach. Something was out there, in the pines clustered along the path. He sensed that the world had changed. The trees no longer seemed alive, and the air was a lifeless miasma. Yet beyond this lack of life, beyond the shadows between the pines, something—moving, yet not living—lurked, and hunted.

In time, the darkness was complete. Thorsten ate a carefully-measured meal of road bread, and prepared his bedroll. There would be no tent; he had one purpose, to get to Adal Vale, and comfort was the least of his concerns. Yet here, at nightfall, there was nothing to protect him from the looming darkness, and often he opened his eyes after sensing something was stirring.

Experience taught him that trying to sleep never worked; the Lady of Dreams had to come to you, by her own accord. The best course of action was to relax. Yet pressure mounted in Thorsten, and he wanted nothing more than the pure light of dawn.

As he lay there, eyes shut, a sound—quiet at first—distinguished itself against the constant moan of the wind. A chittering, like teeth, as if someone were caught ill-prepared in the blizzard.

Thorsten opened his eyes. Through a veil of light snowfall, he made out a silhouette. It was a man's shape, heavy-set and tall. It was not one of the small lowland Badelgarders, nor was it as hulking and huge as a troll. It was Thorsten's size, tall and powerfully-built, like one of the valemen.

Thorsten's axe lay right next to him. He reached for it, grasped the familiar wooden haft, and as it did the silhouette responded in kind, darting toward him.

Thorsten scurried backward, out of the protection of the bedroll and into the snow. He stumbled to his feet, and there, in the moonlight, he laid eyes on his brother.

There was Gunstein—Huge Gunstein, as some called him. He did not look well. He was bald, as normal, but his beard—though present—had turned from black to a bronze color. A closer inspection, as Gunstein stepped awkwardly towards him, revealed that his fingernails had grown abnormally long. Thorsten had never considered Gunstein to have exemplary hygiene, but any sane person would trim nails of that length.

"Brother," Thorsten said, "you do not look well." A heady stench hung about his brother.

Gunstein spoke. "Thorsten." His voice was higher than he remembered, but memory is a cloudy looking-glass. Yellow teeth protruded far beyond his dark gums. "I am so glad to see you."

"You do not seem yourself, brother," Thorsten said, "but indeed I am glad to see you. Gladder than I've ever been to see anyone." And it was true. Thorsten's friends were few by any measure. Now, his own flesh and blood was here, right before him… but he was not the same. He touched Gunstein's hand, and it was cold. Something wasn't right with him. It seemed impossible that a living hand could be that cold. Could he be one of *them* that the rumors spread about? The dead who walked? It did not matter. Living or living dead, his brother was before him.

Thorsten embraced Gunstein. His brother's entire body was cold. The sickening smell for a second overwhelmed him, and he stepped back.

"Where are you going?" Gunstein said. "This road leads into the mountains. You aren't going back to the Vale, are you?"

"I was…" Thorsten read disapproval in Gunstein's oddly sallow eyes.

"You don't really think mother will forgive you, do you?" Gunstein laughed. "She would never forgive us. She is pious to a fault, thinking only of what is in heaven rather than what is on earth."

Thorsten wasn't sure if he agreed with the characterization.

"She would not let you into her house," Gunstein said. "She would send you out in the cold and let you die. Don't expect forgiveness. You have committed crimes she cannot forgive."

"I would not speak of our mother that way," Thorsten said.

"You must come with me." Gunstein's grin was strangely wide, despite his flaccid, drooping skin. "We are still friends. I will be your companion. But do not fool yourself; our mother will never forgive us for the lives we've led."

"Gunstein." As he observed the loose skin, noticing a slight greenish hue despite the lack of light, the transformation of his brother fully dawned on him. "What has happened to you? You are changed."

"A man slew me months ago," Gunstein said. "A swordsman of great skill, a scion of a noble house. Well-trained, well-equipped, and well-born like we never were. He landed a killing blow, but he did not escape with his life."

"You are dead, then. But you talk. How is that possible?"

"Days later I awoke," Gunstein said. "I was surprised at first. I stretched out my fingers… they were strangely numb, but I could move them. I took my first steps. I realized I was more powerful than I ever have been. My meager spirit was replaced with a great intelligence. I realized I could live a life superior to my former self. All Badelgard is at my fingertips… and yours, too, if you will accompany me… brother."

"I… I don't know… Mother—"

"Silence!" Gunstein hissed. "I told you, mother would never have you back. She despises us both. In her mind, we are vagabonds. She would never forgive us. So stop suggesting it."

Thorsten looked down. "I…" He could offer no argument. A weight fell over his heart. If only he had made better decisions. Thorsten and Gunstein—devil-children—killing their stepfather, an upstanding valeman. The few who lived there chased them out, and so they descended into the lowland to live a life of crime. Who could forgive Thorsten? After what they had done, any hatred toward Thorsten was more than deserved, and any love was unwarranted.

He looked down into the quickly-accumulating snow. If Thorsten had done things differently, perhaps it wouldn't have ended like this: the dead of Badelgard refusing to rest in their graves, a dark pall spreading over all things, and a winter that promised to last a lifetime.

"Where shall we go?" Thorsten's voice was quieter and hoarser than he intended.

"Since mother will not accept us," Thorsten said, "I know a place… the few good men in Badelgard left, they are making a last stand. They've hoarded food all summer and autumn. They have enough to last through the winter. I wanted to tell you, my brother, because you are my flesh and blood."

"And how did you find me?" Thorsten wasn't sure he wanted to know the answer.

"In my new state I have powers of great intelligence, but also scent."

His entire manner of speech had changed.

"In my past life you and I were blood-brothers," Gunstein said. "Do you remember our pact?"

Age fourteen. Two cuts. Hand-and-hand. A promise that they would never do harm to each other; and a vow that they would spill the blood of any who harmed the other. Of course, they spilled the blood of many more, and in time even the bond itself was broken. "I remember," Thorsten said.

"Then as blood-brothers, we must go," Thorsten said. "At dawn, follow me. I know you humans need rest."

CHAPTER TWO

When the sun's first rays glanced through the trees, waking Thorsten from his rest, Gunstein stood in the exact same position he had left him. And now, in the brightness of the morning, Thorsten realized how cadaverous his brother looked. To say he did not look well would be inaccurate; he looked dead, and his skin had a sickly green tint. His yellow eyes were soupy. Flies buzzed around him. But he was Thorsten's brother.

He is my brother.

"Are you ready?" Gunstein said.

"I am," Thorsten answered, and at once set about packing his things.

Thorsten guessed they were somewhere in the nebulous border between Trowheim and Ostergard. The snow had accumulated over the night, and now reached the ankle. The sky, for once, was blue and mostly cloudless. But the chill had deepened so much that even in his bearskin cloak, his thick winter cap, and his multiple layers, numbness began to spread through Thorsten's body.

Gunstein was ill-prepared compared to his brother. He wore a light summer kirtle, inappropriate for the harsh weather. The faded green wool was torn in places, the telltale rips where evil wounds had fallen. Despite the lack of clothing, Gunstein did not shiver. Perhaps it was one of the gifts of living death.

"Let us go," Gunstein said.

Thorsten gave one passing glance to the glorious peaks of the Dragonteeth—jagged purple rock half-covered in a sea of green pines—and gave up the hopes of his journey there.

Thorsten followed his brother through a pine thicket. The snow seemed even deeper here, though it was likely just an effect of the thick black boughs.

"What is it like to be dead?" Thorsten said as he pressed through the wall of trees.

"What is it like?" Gunstein's voice had changed in his new state; it was higher, shriller, now. "To live beyond death is the greatest gift of all. It is on the level of godliness. I am a higher being. I am beyond the cares of the mortal world: beyond pain; beyond hunger and lust; beyond the shackles of morality. I wish you could be like me, brother. Maybe you will be, one day."

"I don't want to be," Thorsten answered. "I am happy that you are happy. But I don't want to live beyond death. One life is enough for me. One life of mistakes… one life of murder and theft. I do not want to live again."

"Perhaps you will have no choice," Gunstein said.

Thorsten gulped. He didn't know why his brother had said that. It did not matter. He had to remember that his own brother was with him now; flesh of his flesh, bound together in a blood-pact. He walked with the only person in this world who would forgive him for his crimes, who would call him "friend." They shared entries on the Hangman's List on multiple occasions; and each time, managed to collect enough gold to bribe their way off it. Yes, this bond of brotherhood could never be shaken.

A clearing opened up before them. Gunstein ducked behind some bushes. "Get down!" he hissed.

Thorsten took cover behind the trunk of a spruce. His confusion lasted only a few moments before he realized his brother's purpose. Footsteps echoed through the wintry morning air. Many footsteps.

Out of the veil of the trees something finally emerged. He was perhaps seven feet tall. Black full-plate armor obscured every part of his body. Spikes protruded from the pauldrons, and the images of tortured, groaning faces were painted on the dark steel. From within the giant greathelm, two red eyes peered out like ghostly lights. Rime covered his gauntlets. He wielded a giant sword in both hands, and its blade—a pale white color—glowed with cold. Around this dark warrior, an air of wintry gloom radiated, chilling not just Thorsten's body but also his soul.

Behind this dark champion, a group of underlings marched. There were a dozen in immediate view, but doubtlessly more behind. They were humanoid. If elves, the most twisted and perverted of their race: heavy-set and tall; their chests and faces so hairy they appeared bestial; thick, disheveled beards of copper and brown; and pale yellow eyes.

From the right of the clearing, another group emerged to meet them: a dozen humans. Sons and daughters of Badelgard that had defected, perhaps. Thorsten had no respect for cowards.

"My lord Arani," said a Badelgard man, girt in the chain shirt and hand-axe of a warrior. He knelt.

"Slave." The champion's voice was many-threaded, like a choir. "I have summoned you to this meeting for a purpose. A morguis has broken free of Lady Inana's control. You humans are too weak to dispose of a morguis, but if you find it you will tell us. We cannot have an insurrection of the living dead. They were created by our wizards. They are slaves like you, even if they are far more useful. Do you understand?"

"Yes!" the Badelgard man shouted. "Yes, my lord. I will do whatever I can, as always. Long live the Great Witch and her supreme goddess."

"The morguis is the paramount achievement of necromancy," the champion said. "No other civilization has discovered the means of making them. Despite their vast power, they have a weakness: intelligence. If you find the morguis, inform me at once. If you do not, I shall dispose of you in the most painful way possible. Your torture will last years."

"Yes! Yes!" the Badelgard man cried. "Long live the Great Witch and her supreme goddess!"

The champion turned around. The dark army departed. The

humans turned and went their own way. Thorsten remained silent and unmoving; Gunstein waited several minutes before his brother stood up and motioned for him to do the same.

As he stood up, waves of nausea coursed through Thorsten. "What in Varda was that?"

Gunstein's yellow eyes widened. "The man in armor is one of the Sorelden."

"Sorelden?"

"You humans call them Ulfr."

You are human, too. Thorsten shivered.

"His black war-plate means he is a Fell Lord. A tiny handful of Sorelden males survive the necromantic transformation. Those that do are girt in the dark armor, and given rime-frost blades. A wound from a Fell Lord's sword cannot be mended except by the healing masters of Danarion..."

How much my brother has changed, Thorsten reflected. He and his brother were as uneducated as they came. Where and what Danarion was, he had no idea, but it sounded Elvish. In life, Gunstein would never know such things. Of the two brothers, Thorsten had been considered the smartest; yet in a crowd of lowland Badelgarders he was always the least intelligent.

The conversation between the Ulfr lord and the human slaves did nothing to ease him. What had they spoken of? A "morguis"... some kind of twisted Ulfr creation. It had broken free of its controls. It was dangerous. It was the most powerful of the undead.

As he looked into his brother's soupy yellow eyes, long-devoid of life, a chill settled over him. *Is my brother the morguis?*

CHAPTER THREE

What was a morguis? Why was it dangerous? Undead were walking corpses… how could they differ in strength? If his brother was, indeed, the morguis, were his words of affection insincere? Was he luring Thorsten to his death?

The chief question remained: What was a morguis? As he struggled through the windblown snow, Thorsten began to wonder if he should turn back while he had the chance. Mother would never forgive him; Gunstein, morguis or no, had convinced him of that. He did not deserve forgiveness. But perhaps Adal Vale would be a good place to retire, to let the forces of justice bring about his end. He was a valeman in a world of halflings, and perhaps he should die as one. At the very least, he could tell his mother how she had been right all along; he had made poor decisions and ruined himself, and she could say, "I told you so."

"Where is this hideout?" Thorsten said. "Who is there, and how do you know about it?"

Gunstein halted his lumbering steps and turned around. His eyes narrowed. "Don't ask questions, brother. Trust me in my new form; I am wise, and know the proper paths to take."

"What if I want to know?" Thorsten snapped. He laid a hand on his axe haft.

"Do not touch that weapon!" A shrill screech, completely unlike his brother and, perhaps, not altogether human.

"What is our mother's name?" Thorsten would not be daunted.

"What?" Gunstein's eyes narrowed further. "Why do you ask this?"

"I want to know if you're really my brother, or if you are someone using my brother's body."

Gunstein bared his teeth. They protruded far beyond his black gums. "Our mother is Gerta. Our father—rest his soul—is Bjarn son of Adalf. Do you have any more questions, brother?"

"What was our dog's name?"

"Aron," Gunstein hissed. "Big, even for a mountain dog. You rode him when you were little… fell off every time. Satisfied?"

The memory brought a half-grin to Thorsten's lips, but it vanished instantly. "All right. I'm satisfied, brother."

But in truth, he was not.

Gunstein turned and, together, they continued their journey through the thick stands of spruce, the frozen streams and the drifts of snow. Each step was reluctant. Still, he clung to the hope that his brother's soul remained inside him; yet this hope, tenuous already, faded fast.

CHAPTER FOUR

They did not cease their march until night fell. In darkness, a heavy snow began. Thorsten ate the last of the road-bread. He set his bedroll out. Gunstein stood and watched.

"I will make a fire," Thorsten said.

"I hate fire."

"You *what?*" Telling Thorsten not to bother wouldn't rouse any suspicion, but stating it in those terms was downright strange.

"Don't make one," Gunstein said. "That's final."

"Am I your brother or your slave?"

Gunstein snarled. "I would not risk my anger."

"Again. Am I your brother or your slave?"

Gunstein roared and ran at him. Thorsten clambered to his feet and readied his axe. Before he could pitch it back, Gunstein struck him across the jaw with such force that he toppled over into the snow.

Before he could reach for the axe his brother was on top of him, pinning his arms into the snow, filling Thorsten's nostrils with his fetid stench. "I said not to risk my anger. It was a warning. Next time, I won't hold back."

Thorsten bit back a caustic reply. This was not his brother. His brother Gunstein was violent when roused, a burglar and a vagabond. But he would never threaten Thorsten.

"Don't even think of escaping in the night," Gunstein hissed. "I can follow scents for miles off. Your brother was stupid but I am not."

"And who are you?"

The monster spit in Thorsten's face. The moisture was thick, adhesive, and smelled fouler than a thousand rotting corpses. "You will come with me. You will not ask questions; it is beneath me to answer them. To answer your question: no, you are not my brother. You are my slave, my catch, my game, and I shall do what I like with you. Try to resist me, and you will regret your decision."

In the monster's yellow eyes, Thorsten glimpsed a different

person, a new intelligence: primitive yet cunning, remorseless and predatory, superhuman yet grossly subhuman. Waves of revulsion pulsed through Thorsten's body; he flipped over and vomited into the snow.

Was this the morguis that they spoke of? It did not matter. Whatever intelligence had overtaken his brother, it posed incredible danger to Thorsten. Escaping would take more wit than a lumbering valeman would ever possess. Thorsten was not the equal of this undead monster, morguis or otherwise.

Thorsten wept into his bedroll. Eventually sleep took him.

The morning light illuminated a new reality. Things looked much the same: thick snow, spruces and pines, and wilderness all around. But "Gunstein"—not having slept at any point in the night—stared at Thorsten as he woke from his slumber. Unmoving as a statue, yellow eyes open wide and reflecting no human emotion. Thorsten would have to fight this monster, morguis or no, but he had to use caution. He had no doubt that the creature's threats were not idle; it would not give Thorsten an easy death.

He could only stare in those sallow eyes for a fleeting second. Quickly he looked down and at once set about packing his things. Then he stowed his axe across his back. Surprisingly "Gunstein" made no quarrel, but perhaps this creature was confident in its power. It made sense—if this were the deadly creation called the morguis—that it had nothing to fear from a steel axe-bit splitting its head.

Thorsten moved slowly and reluctantly through the snow, covered in gooseflesh and nauseous. Where was this creature taking him? Certainly not to any safe haven, as it initially promised. If it was the escaped morguis, then it would not take him to its Ulfr creators either. If it wanted to devour Thorsten, then why hadn't it acted by now?

It was a mystery he did not want to ponder.

As the march went on, it became evident they were headed north. Likely they were somewhere in Trowheim, and Blackhelm Keep, therefore, was not far-off. But trouble had fallen upon Badelgard. The Ulfr—risen from the dead by some black spell—walked freely among the humans. Thorsten doubted the Earl of Trowheim had any power to save him. Their nation was doomed to an eternal winter and a mustering of the restless dead.

Onward they went. The false Gunstein marched fast, taking unnaturally long strides. When Thorsten fell behind, the monster threatened to bind him with a collar and tie him to a leash. The more Thorsten thought about it, and the more exhausted he became, the better getting dragged across the snow began to sound.

Yet he continued at the hurried pace. At noon, famished and exhausted, Thorsten cried out, "I need to eat!" and fell to his knees.

"There is no food," the false Gunstein said, "and if there were, I would not let you have it. Now get up and keep moving, or I will make you yearn for Hell."

"I already do!" Thorsten growled. He began to reach for his axe but quickly thought better of it. It was not the right time, not the right place.

"Believe me, I can make things much worse on you. You are testing my patience. Get up now!"

Thorsten let out a shrill scream as he obeyed. His legs were jelly, only barely supporting his weight. He staggered on, more sluggishly than ever before. False Gunstein slowed his pace, but it was a matter of practicality; compassion was alien to him, now.

The sun dipped low. The northern mountains appeared, the roof of the world. Jagged purple, capped in snow like their brethren in the east. Thorsten had once loved these peaks. He had once loved many things, but now all he could think about was the hulk lumbering in front of him; his own brother, changed after death and given false life. Seeing Gunstein's body—green, giving way to rot yet animate—sent more waves of revulsion through him.

Then, as a chill wind blew out of the mountains and sent stinging snow into Thorsten's eyes, the false Gunstein shouted out, "The Ulfr are near! Hurry, brother!"

"I am *not* your brother!" Thorsten again reached for his axe, and again drew back his hand. A question presented itself to him, now: *would I rather the Ulfr kill me, or this soulless mockery of my brother?* It took only seconds before Thorsten decided to slow his stagger, and then to stand still.

Gunstein turned around. His eyes bulged, and though dead and watery, infinite rage burned behind them. "Hurry, or I will make you yearn for Hell!"

"I already do," Thorsten hissed, and—grabbing the wooden haft—readied his axe. It had served him well in battle, and it would serve him well now. Or so he hoped.

Gunstein ran at him. Thorsten dove into the trees just as a group of Ulfr emerged from the trees.

"There it is! The morguis!" The Fell Lord was not with them. A few members of the Ulfr party wore iron caps, but most had little armor. This granted them mobility, Thorsten noted as his false brother's attention diverted to the warriors.

The morguis darted at them with the speed and reflexes of a mountain cat. One Ulfr warrior, unencumbered, dodged out of the way. Another was less lucky; the morguis slammed its shoulder into him. The Ulfr went flying and hit a tree with a back-breaking and trunk-splintering crack.

Just as Thorsten noticed one Ulfr with a bow, an arrow flew at the morguis. It stuck deep into its back, but seemed to do no harm. Thorsten's brother, the morguis, tackled another Ulfr warrior and rent his ribcage with its fist.

A purple tentacle-like thing began to wriggle out of his brother's nose. Whether the sight sent him over the edge or if he quickly thought better of watching the battle, it did not matter; Thorsten turned and took off into the dark woods at a sprint. *Please, gods,* he prayed, *I am not worthy of an answered prayer. But let the Ulfr defeat my brother the morguis.*

Cloud cover and new snowfall quickened the coming night. The air was dead and still as Thorsten sprinted through darkness, fearing no bear or White Wolf, fearing only his brother's dead yellow eyes and the evil that had overtaken his mind. With or without his mother's forgiveness, he should never have accompanied Gunstein. But if he had refused, the morguis would not let its prey go so easily.

As the sky darkened and night closed in, Thorsten's exhaustion caught up with him. His sprint slowed to a jog and then to a stagger. The forced march had drained all his energy. Here he was, in the wilds of Trowheim. A wide swath of land separated him from Oskir; and who knew if it remained a human city? The Ulfr now wandered Badelgard freely, growing in strength by the day. What human warrior could match the strength of a Fell Lord?

Despite his exhaustion, Thorsten kept moving. He could not— he *would* not—be captured by the morguis again. The Ulfr, for all their dark magic and the evil customs that lived on in legend, did not seem as cruel or inhuman as the morguis. And though Thorsten kept up his stagger, he knew that in the darkness behind him, the false Gunstein— fuming at his failure—would resume the hunt as soon as possible.

A chill wind blew out of the west. Snow began to fall. Thorsten guessed it was midnight but there was no way to tell. The moon—seen only in fleeting glimpses among the shifting silver clouds—was full and bright white. In Adal Vale, Thorsten's grandfather had spun tales of men changing into bears by the light of the full moon. What a great gift that would be right now, Thorsten mused. As a valeman, he knew full well that bears were swift, that they could outrun a human and perhaps a morguis. Bears were deadly, but they were noble, and the valemen respected them above all beasts.

The winds tossed the snow into a blinding powder. Thorsten's body grew numb. He continued through it because he would prefer Lady Winter's deadly embrace to ever seeing the morguis again. But more than cold, he was growing exhausted—more exhausted than he had ever been—yet the mental image of the morguis drove him forward harder than a cattle prod.

At some ungodly hour, a distinct noise emerged out of the snow. At first, rustling bushes—and Thorsten at once thought of the morguis—but then bells, and the huffing of a horse. A shrill voice called out something in a language he did not recognize. Thorsten quickened his pace. But soon the vast shape of a horse and its rider overtook him.

For a second, the silvery clouds parted, and the moon spread its light all over the wilderness. A woman rode on the horse: an Ulfr woman, her black hair tied in a bun and her skin strangely hairless in comparison to her male brethren. Her robe was black and silken, with a rigid collar, and embroidered with skulls. Her large yellow eyes focused intensely on Thorsten. Then, after the instant's illumination, the silvery clouds covered up the moon, and she was once again a black shape against the trees.

"Who are you?" she said in the Badelgardic tongue.

"Thorsten son of Bjarn," he replied, and realized he feared her less than his false brother. "Who are you?"

She did not reply. She turned and shouted something in her own tongue.

Then—a harbinger of his presence—gooseflesh covered Thorsten's skin, and heavy iron steps heralded the coming of Arani, the Fell Lord. Against the darkness, the red fires of his eyes appeared. In the same many-stranded choir of voices, he spoke—of all things—in the human tongue: "Killing him would be most unwise, Lady Inana. The morguis has marked him as its prey. We should use him as a lure."

"That is wise," Lady Inana replied. "The morguis is the pinnacle of Sorelden achievement. It is unfortunate they are so proud and intelligent; but it is in the larva's nature."

Larva. A word Thorsten had heard before, yet did not know its meaning.

"I must regain control of the morguis very soon," Lady Inana said. "That much is clear. Left by itself it can wreak great havoc. But in the end, our struggle is minor. The Seat of the Great Mother is nearly out of the ice. Our armies roam freely across the land. We have slaughtered humans in droves. In time, the rebel undead will fall under our sway… with me, or without me."

Arani took a few more heavy iron steps toward his lady. A cold like nothing Thorsten remembered filled him, covered him in gooseflesh and chilled his soul. He wanted nothing more than the fell blade through his heart; but instead, he would be lure to the morguis.

CHAPTER FIVE

If—in the bright light of the morning—the Ulfr were surprised by the morguis' absence, they were not any more surprised than Thorsten. As he struggled to sleep, he had no doubt that his brother the morguis would find him, defeat this party of Ulfr, and drag him to its hellish den. But here he was, alive. The sun shone brightly upon the glittering white snow. The sky was bright blue and nearly cloudless. The day would have seemed hopeful if the Fell Lord Arani did not loom above him: a grim statue of black steel, his white blade pulsing with a cold that pierced the mind.

Thorsten wanted to beg the Fell Lord to slay him. But he doubted that pity ever motivated the Ulfr. Surely, if he pleaded with Arani, the Fell Lord would only wish to prolong his suffering.

Thorsten took in slow, deep breaths. The aura surrounding Arani seemed to deaden the air, and make each inhalation twice more difficult. He sat up from his bedroll, now covered in rime frost. The Ulfr lady Inana had dismounted from her horse. Now, in the light of day, Thorsten could see her fully. Her deep eyes—though yellow—would be the envy of Badelgard woman; her wavy black hair, tied into a bun, somehow reflected nobility. Her staff, made of gnarled dark wood, and topped with a skull-shaped gem, was doubtlessly an implement of magic. She was an Ulfr witch, a necromancer, a disturber of the dead.

"Has the morguis lost the scent?" Arani's red eyes flared brightly and dimmed just as quickly.

"A morguis will never abandon its quarry," said Lady Inana. "To the exclusion of all other things, it focuses on its chosen prey… even though your soldiers' flesh is just as savory for its young, it will not abandon this *Thorsten*."

Feeding its young—a thought Thorsten wished had never crossed his mind. But what were the young of a morguis? Thorsten had a difficult time imagining a litter of false Gunsteins, each yellow-eyed, rotting and green like their parent. No matter how he pictured it, the thought sickened him.

And the thought of being fed to the ungodly litter… gnawed and devoured, slowly.

He retched.

"Perhaps we should go west," Arani suggested. "If we draw close, perhaps he will take in our scent."

"Never underestimate a morguis." Lady Inana ran her fingers along the warped wood of her staff. "It will come for its quarry. It will die to find its quarry. It will find Thorsten's scent in time, and we must be prepared for it. If we journey toward the morguis, we may be caught unawares, and that will spell our end. Capturing the pinnacle creation of Sorelda, and returning it to my control, is no easy task. Preparation is key."

Arani bowed his helmeted head. "Yes, Your Worship."

Lady Inana and Thorsten exchanged glances. How deep, how bright yellow were her eyes. Yet Thorsten saw no life in them, nor any compassion. Keeping him alive was no act of mercy; if they let him die, they would lose their lure. If they lost their lure, they would lose control of the morguis. And once they gained control, who knows what would happen? A stroke from Arani's blade, spilling Thorsten's innards all over the snow? Or would they let the morguis—now under their control—have its quarry, and feed Thorsten to its young?

He retched again.

A few hours passed. Thorsten's stomach growled. He couldn't remember the last time he ate. The road-bread had run out long ago, or so it seemed. He glanced at Inana. The dark lady was looking at him.

"The giant is hungry." Inana pursed her lips. "We must not let him go to waste. But food for the dead is not fit for the living." Her eyes, for a moment, seemed to glow. "Arani, you have a bit of the *honthal amani* left over from your long slumber. It is useless to you now. Let him have it."

"As you wish, milady," Arani said. He removed a small cask from his belt and handed it to Thorsten.

Thorsten took it. No sane person—valeman or Badelgarder—would accept a gift from the Ulfr. But how could it harm him? If they wanted to kill him, they would have done it by now. He unplugged the stopper—made of coarse bone—and drank whatever was inside.

The liquor was harsh, but it filled him with warmth. Within the span of a few moments, his hunger vanished, too. He handed the cask back to Arani. "Thank you."

"It has taken away your hunger," Inana said, "and it has made your scent more powerful to the morguis. In this, we have both received what we desire." She smiled, revealing mangled yellow teeth. Her eyes remained the same as always: bright yellow, beautiful and enchanting, yet without life.

It was late afternoon when things began to stir in the makeshift camp. Thorsten watched as his companions—Arani, the Fell Lord, and his lady-liege—moved from their posts, looking into the forest as an icy gale blew down from the mountains. Powdery snow blinded Thorsten's vision, but a familiar scent of rot reached his nose. In the western sky, silver clouds had begun to roll in, veiling the sun.

Through the black cover of pines and the whirling snow, Thorsten made out a dark shape. Hulking, seven feet tall: a morguis inhabiting the body of Gunstein. Even from this distance, its fetid stench had begun to overwhelm him.

Inana crouched and bent her staff forward, assuming an offensive stance. Lord Arani took several heavy iron strides in front of his lady and drew his white blade. Thorsten grabbed his axe from the ground, where his captors had left it lying. He reminded himself that he was not fighting for the Ulfr; he was fighting for his own survival, and these two champions of darkness were only temporary allies.

The morguis took its first lumbering steps.

Inana shouted something at it.

"I have assumed the body of a human!" The morguis roared his reply. "I will only answer in the human tongue."

"Very well, worm!" Inana shouted. "I am your master because I gave you life. I brought you out of ignorance, out of the mindless morass of vermin-kind. Once you were a maggot, the wicked spawn of a fly. It is I who brought you into intelligence, and it is I who gave you your pride! *Submit to me!*"

The morguis shrieked. "Out of my mind, witch! It does not matter that you created me. I am superior, now, to you and all others who walk on two feet. You must submit to *me*. Now give me my prey, or I will destroy you and your companion."

Inana thrust her staff forward. Wind burst from her, and in its wake, an air of power filled the forest. The morguis shrieked again, shriller than before. "Listen to me, vermin!" Inana screamed. "Listen to me, worm! Surrender to your creator. Surrender to your master. I have given you your strength and your sentience, and I can take it away. Remember that your mother was a fly. Remember that, at heart, you are a maggot!"

Thorsten retched. If she spoke the truth, it was more disgusting than he had ever envisioned. A maggot, given intelligence and life through fell powers… was that a morguis?

It shrieked as it charged toward Lady Inana. Thorsten recognized the struggle about to ensue. He had to make the best of it. In either party's company, he would die. If he—now nourished back to health from Arani's liquor—could run far enough away, perhaps he could find safe haven. Perhaps he would not go to Adal Vale; perhaps he'd go to the southlands, soft as they were, free of the fell winter and the armies of darkness that roamed Badelgard.

He sprinted into the darkness of the pines. Inana continued her shouted exhortations. Even as Thorsten fled the air of her magic, it remained around him for many hundreds of yards.

CHAPTER SIX

The light of the sun dwindled. Thorsten continued his sprint as long as he could sustain it, but not much time passed before he slowed to a stagger. His throat burned and his lungs were taxed to their absolute limit; his legs could barely sustain a walk. Not even the fear of the morguis could drive him any faster. His body wouldn't allow it.

He hacked and coughed, and his throat was so hoarse that breathing in the cold air filled him with pain. As the sun set and darkness flooded in, and the snowfall picked up, he wondered if he should give in. But all he had to do was picture those yellow eyes and he found the energy to continue the stagger.

At last the darkness was complete; a fetid stench filled his nostrils and Thorsten realized he had fallen face-first in the snow. He looked up and saw the half-rotted body of Gunstein. The morguis was here. He vomited.

The hulking giant, mock image of his dear brother Gunstein, hauled Thorsten into its putrid arms. A rotten stench filled Thorsten's nostrils as the morguis spoke: "I've found my prey."

Thorsten, now, had discovered how his life would end: as food for the spawn of the morguis, nibbled and gnawed alive until only bone remained. But it would end; that was enough consolation. Through all the bites and the horrid pains, he would remind himself that it would end. Hell would await him, a fitting punishment for his crimes. But Hell could not possibly be worse than this.

Thorsten fell asleep in the putrid arms. When he awoke, perhaps he would find himself in the morguis' den.

In the red light of dawn, Thorsten realized that the morguis had carried him to the foot of the mountains. With long strides, it ascended a steep incline with its former brother in tow. The peaks, covered in snow, appeared directly above him. In the blood-red sun, he realized his axe remained clipped to his belt. The morguis had nothing to fear from such simple weapons, or so it seemed.

"The Sorelden have lost our trail." Somehow it knew Thorsten was awake. "When we reach my nest, you must not struggle against the younglings. You certainly do not have the power to slay them, but they are weaker than me."

Only an alien mind—one that did not understand human emotions—would make such a suggestion. Perhaps a morguis felt no pain, or did not fear death. The thought sickened him.

Thorsten grabbed his axe, ripped it from his belt. The morguis moved with imperceptible swiftness, swiped the weapon out of Thorsten's hand and cast it onto the snow. It skidded down the mountainside and then was still.

The last hope, gone. The gods had decided: Thorsten would be food for the morguis' younglings. He fell still and determined to struggle no more.

Thorsten awoke as they approached the mouth of a cave. The sounds of shrill hisses and wriggling echoed from within. Thorsten's heart stirred from his slumber; his blood went cold as he drew closer to his doom. He writhed in the morguis' grip, struggling against the iron strength of its hands. At last—whether by chance or his own guile— Thorsten fell headlong into the snow and out of the morguis' grip.

He ran down the mountainside, letting the incline speed him along, but within seconds the same putrid hand gripped his wrist.

"Surrender," the morguis hissed, and dragged him toward the mouth of the cave.

The sun spread its rays only partially into the cave, but that was enough to grant dim light. A few feet in, the stone ground gave way to a precipitous drop. Within the pit, Thorsten caught sight of the monster's young.

Where one of them ended and another began, Thorsten could not tell. In truth, the thousands and thousands of them formed one wriggling, writhing mass. Individually, they appeared—in some ways—like the maggots one finds in spoiled meat. But a closer inspection revealed mouths full of tiny needle-sharp teeth, and as they wriggled and hissed, it became clear that they were starving.

"My babies," the morguis whispered. "They will fight over you. The strongest one will burrow into you and assume your mind. My child and I... existing in the bodies of two brothers. I can't think of anything that will bring me more joy. I will be united with my child, both in mind and in body. No other morguis is so lucky."

A wave of cold air fled through the cave mouth. The morguis larva in the pit let out a collective shriek, and their wriggling became even more frantic. The sight sickened Thorsten even more and he vomited again.

Arani appeared at the cave mouth. In one hand, he held his white blade. In the other, he held Thorsten's axe. "Your quarry left me a token. Without his guile, I would never have located your den!"

The morguis screamed. It slammed its fist into Thorsten, and he went flying into the pit of vermin.

CHAPTER SEVEN

The pit was dark, and for a while the only thing Thorsten sensed was his own revulsion. A thousand—no, a million—bodies wriggled against his skin. In time, minor piercing pains began to sting him.

With each sting they appeared to pierce deeper and deeper. He screamed. Perhaps—Thorsten thought in the pain's delirium—it was as the morguis said. These maggots from Hell now competed with each other to assume Thorsten's mind. Which one had the strength to burrow deep into his skin? Whose teeth were the sharpest, and which vermin's muscles allowed for the most penetrating bite? Thorsten would not wait to find out.

In the haze of pain he struggled to his feet. He was waist-deep in the writhing maggots, and several clung to his arms and face, attempting to burrow but unable to use their siblings for momentum. Through this sea of maggots, Thorsten waded up to the cliff face, but it was too tall, and handholds nonexistent.

Up above him, on this surface, the Fell Lord did battle with the morguis. His white blade shone with a frigid gleam as he struck at the rebellious undead. By now, Lady Inana had appeared in her black witch robes. Perhaps they had given up on their quest to control the fiend. Its mind was too strong, or perhaps too alien. Now, as their duty to the dark queen of the Ulfr, the witch commanded her champion to cut the morguis down before it wrought havoc on its creators.

A pain sharper than any Thorsten had ever experienced throttled his body, his muscles, his mind. One of the morguis younglings had finally pierced his thigh deep enough. At this instant the others stopped; out of all these thousands and thousands, one had proven itself strong enough to overtake Thorsten's mind.

The pain, however, did not stop. Instead, as the morguis larva burrowed through Thorsten's muscles, shredding through the sinews with its maw of needles, the pain nearly incapacitated him. But he would not resign himself to this fate. He leapt again and again, trying to reach the top of the cliff face.

Yet the higher he went, the more impossible the task seemed. Even at seven feet tall—giant valeman that he was—the tips of his fingers brushed against the sheer stone.

Up above, the Fell Lord swept past the morguis' arm, and a sudden strike from his enemy sent the white blade clattering to the stone ground. The undead monster, most prized creation of Ulfr-kind, had grown too powerful for its creators. With a hammering fist, it knocked the Fell Lord—in spite of the plates of black armor—to the ground. It leapt upon him and went in for the kill.

Thorsten focused his mind and leapt higher than he ever had. This time his fingers brushed the surface. At the same time, a spasm of pain shuddered through his body like never before. The maggot was working his way up the leg. His screams echoed through the cave.

He steeled himself, crouched down, and leapt with all the strength that remained. He laid hold of the cave floor and little by little—as more spasms of pain filled him—he pulled himself to the surface.

The morguis had torn off the Fell Lord's helmet, revealing a rotted face, and laid its fingers upon him. Hungry, perhaps, or just desirous of seeing its enemy in pain, it was distracted. The Fell Lord's white blade lay on the ground.

Thorsten scrambled to it and grasped the leather hilt. It burned his hands, searing his flesh with cold. He pitched it back, ran forward, and clove the white metal through his brother's skull, down his spine and across his back, and finally dropped the fell blade onto the ground.

He glanced at his fingers, burnt with white flame. His brother's entire body had come apart. A foul stench filled the cave, so thick and miasmic Thorsten could feel it against his skin. His brother's skull, rent-open, revealed the contents of his brain.

There, residing within, was the morguis: ancient parasite, ridged and purple, without eyes or limbs. If a maggot, the largest of all its kind. Vicious, but—now separated from the body it controlled—powerless.

What was its name? Thorsten wasn't sure. The sight of this primitive wyrm, given power by ancient magic or alchemy, filled Thorsten with panic. His axe lay there, too, alongside the dead Fell Lord. He would not touch the white blade again. He hurried toward it and grabbed the haft.

The witch still stood at the cave entrance, struck motionless by awe.

Thorsten pitched back his axe and hammered it into the ancient wyrm's flesh. "What is your name?" he cried, though he didn't know why. The morguis was dead. Perhaps his brother could now find rest… if not in Heaven, then in Hell.

The pain in his leg had stopped. Perhaps the white blade, searing Thorsten with cold, had also killed the child-morguis. He had no time to think about it.

He rushed past the dark lady, knocking her over, and leapt upon her horse. He would ride to Adal Vale, all night if he had to. Even if his mother would never forgive him, it did not matter. He would tell her he was sorry, that she was right. Most importantly of all, he would see her face before this fell winter consumed them all.

He rode down the mountainside, going south. He did not know the way, but if he continued in one direction he would eventually come to a road. Undeveloped though Badelgard was, many roads branched through it. One led east from Oskir: it went to Blackfold, home of superstition and wolves, but also—along another branch—into the high valley where Thorsten's people lived.

He rode all day and all night. In time he reached the road and turned east. The witch's steed, a black mare, was swift and hardy. Perhaps it, too, was dead, but that was of no concern to Thorsten. He would ride her until he reached the Vale, his ancient home, or until he died.

Morning broke. The mountain road wound slowly upward. Thorsten had not been here since he was a boy. But slowly—in spite of the deep snow, nearly reaching the saddle—he began to recognize things. He remembered the place where he'd spent his formative years, these mountains: the twisted peak they called the Horn of Daggir; the point where the incline reversed, and the road gently wound its way into a wide open valley.

There was Adal Vale, and it looked just as he remembered. The pastures, now filled with snow, surrounding the small village center. The buildings were large enough to fit the giants who lived within. The inn, largest of the buildings, still lay in the center; Thorsten wondered if Olaf Black-Beard still served mead to the patrons there.

Gently, Thorsten dismounted. He brushed the mare's thick black mane. "You have done well," he told her. "Now go. Thank you for your help."

The beast turned and galloped back the way it had come. Thorsten turned and walked toward the village center and to the house where, long ago, he had lived.

The few people wandering the village streets—those hardy enough or foolish enough to brave the winter's cold—did not recognize Thorsten. For the most part, he was pleased about that. Perhaps they would not remember him as the bad seed, one of the twins that committed parricide so many years ago. Alden the Shoemaker had grown old and gray, and Metild's youthful beauty had faded. But Thorsten had changed too: perhaps for the better, perhaps for the worse.

At the door of his childhood home he hesitated. What if his mother did not forgive him? He had committed a crime worthy of his own execution. His real father Bjarn had died when he was young... his mother had remarried. His drunkard stepfather had beaten Thorsten for the most minor disappointments. The rage in young Thorsten had simmered a long time before reaching a boil. But, at last, anger had taken over. With Gunstein's help he grabbed a knife… committed parricide. And for that Thorsten deserved execution.

His mother was a good woman. If she did not forgive him, that was her right. If she never let Thorsten into her house, that was her right, and perhaps her duty. Countless years had passed since that awful night. She might never forgive him. But Thorsten wanted to tell her he was sorry.

If she slammed the door in his face, he would understand. If she forgave him, it would be an incomprehensible act. But regardless of it all, Thorsten knew what he had to do. He had to say he was sorry. His mother was a good woman.

He knocked on the door, and waited.

PART TWO:
QUEEN OF NOTHING

CHAPTER ONE

Alysse's glimpse of Heaven had not lasted long. She was back in the mortal world now. Back in the winter's grasp, in the middle of the cold, on her back, and the Golden House... the Golden House was burning.

Faces. So many faces all around her. The people of Oskir hovered above her as she took in her surroundings. Some faces were handsome, and others were not. All of them looked in need. They needed a guide through these harsh times, through this forever winter.

"Queen!" a yellow-toothed woman cried out. "All hail Queen Alysse!"

"All hail Queen Alysse!" the crowd shouted.

Alysse sat up. She was High Queen... she had accomplished her goal. The people of Oskir announced it. But what was she queen of? The Golden House was burning. Harald was dead. The Ulfr walked again in full view of the living. Food was doubtlessly running out. The kingdom lay in shambles... but she was queen.

She stood up weakly. The high hill overlooked the city of Oskir. The commons, the lowborn, had broken through the barriers and entered the king's area.

Memories flooded back to her. She had brought in an army of evil intent. She had ridden across the seas, accompanied by the dark-hearted Jourmande. His knights remained, promising to divvy up Badelgard among themselves. A black time had fallen over Badelgard, and the fault—at least, partially—rested on Alysse.

"Queen Alysse! All hail Queen Alysse!" the crowd roared.

Alysse feigned a smile. "Thank you... thank you, my people. I will lead as best I know how. I will return things to how they were."

How could she? How could anything ever return to the ways they were? The Ulfr had ravaged the whole of the land. The structure of society had irrevocably broken. Even if—after a miracle—the Ulfr threat faded, it would never be the same. Nothing would ever be the same.

"All hail Queen Alysse!"

If Alysse was to be a good queen, the answer would not lie in Badelgard. No. She would have to lead them away from this cursed land. She would have to leave the kingdom she loved. They would lead poor, desperate lives as refugees. They would wander Zarubain like the gypsies, having no home. Not even Alysse's family would accept them as serfs… not after what she had done.

"All hail Queen Alysse!"

The crowd's passion had not faded even slightly. Alysse feigned another smile. "Thank you, my people… thank you!" she repeated. "You've been through much hardship. Things are not the same. Food is short and a dark winter is approaching. I am sorry, my people. I have to make a difficult choice. We must leave… We must leave Badelgard…"

"Leave Badelgard?" a young man in torn, dull clothing asked. What teeth he had were rotten. "It's all we've ever known!"

"You are not warriors," Alysse said in as kind a tone as she could manage. "The Ulfr have overrun the land. If I did not choose to leave, I'd be a poor queen. I don't want to see you suffer as the winter comes… food will soon grow short. If we stay, we won't last long. Leaving is not my first choice, but it is the only one I see before us."

A few frowned. But behind the disappointment, Alysse saw that they knew the truth.

"We will go to the King's Drawbridge. I am the sole ruler of Badelgard now. The guardian of the drawbridge will answer to me…"

A young boy spoke. "And where will we go?" His voice quaked as he shivered and pulled his gray cloak tight. "The horse peoples are savage… they would never give us safe haven!"

Alysse smiled. "You are a wise boy. The answer is simple: we are not going to the horse peoples. We will go south, or east, or north. We will go to Zarubain or some far-flung citadel. It is better than dying."

"I'm not sure it is," the young boy answered.

Alysse's smile only grew. "You are wise beyond your years. But I am queen, and that is my pronouncement. How many of you are there?

A few hundred? The journey to the drawbridge is only twenty miles, if that. We can manage it in a day, if the gods smile on us."

"The gods will not smile on us." The woman's voice was thick and syrupy. Her white eyes indicated she was blind. Amulets of bone hung from her neck, inscribed with runes Alysse did not recognize. "The Ulfr wander the land freely," the woman continued. "A war-band under the command of Varanas, Fell Lord, marches to Oskir as we speak. It is no matter. You are right. We must depart at once."

"And how do you know this?" Alysse had a hunch.

"I once was a witch," the woman answered. "I once loved the Ulfr, but I have seen their evil now. Yet still, they haunt my dreams... I know their plans. I will help you if you will allow it."

"What is your name?" Alysse demanded.

"My name was once Hjorda. The Ulfr, they call me *Cana* now... She-Bear in our tongue."

What was the right course of action? This *Cana* could be of help, if she spoke the truth. If she had truly abandoned her Ulfr lieges, and knew their plans, she would be invaluable.

"You may come with us," Alysse said, "under one condition."

"I'm listening."

"You will call yourself Hjorda, as you were before the evil entered your heart. You will listen to the Ulfr plans, and you will share them with me. I will tolerate a witch in my presence." Alysse harshened her tone. "But if I, at any point, suspect bad faith or treason... if I, at any point, suspect you are communicating with your dark lieges... I will punish you according to our ancient law. Of old, our forebears burned the witches who survived to adulthood. It is a cruel law, and one I disagree with strongly; but the hottest flame in the world is a small price to pay for treason. It is the lowest of crimes."

"I understand, my queen," Hjorda answered. She knelt to the ground. Her robes were tattered and dull brown, but Alysse's dress—once a finely-tailored example of Zarube couture—didn't look any better.

"If you understand, I permit you to accompany us on our journey to the Drawbridge." Alysse looked at the men in the group. They composed less than half the crowd; most had gone to war but they had not. "Men, what few of you there are, I do not permit any of you to leave unarmed. Scour the whole city if you need to. You all must wield a sword or an axe. And women, too, in these dark times you must be armed as well, but I will not force it upon you like the men."

The sun was still bright as they left, but as winter drew near the days would grow shorter and shorter. A thin layer of snow covered the ground and the southeastward-leading road, but high wooden markers revealed their path. To the north and northeast, Alysse could make out the shape of the mountains, a faint gray haze from this distance.

Alysse rode at the vanguard. A good ruler led from the front. If an Ulfr war-band rushed in from the east and slaughtered them all, she would face them first, like the rightful queen of Badelgard. Before she left the City of Kings, she had robbed the corpse of vile Logrin. Now, his longsword—a masterwork of steel—hung from Alysse's side in a leather sheath.

In late afternoon, an eastward wind caused dark clouds to roll in. But even before they had obscured the sun, the light began to fade. Alysse guessed they had traveled five miles down the road, and thanks to the clouds, night would arrive prematurely.

Even against the sound of the wind, the whimpering of Hjorda echoed through the air. Not whimpering, Alysse soon realized, but babbling.

"They are coming... they are coming..."

Alysse looked back. The hundred refugees—perhaps the last humans left in Badelgard—shivered as they followed her. Hjorda looked up at Alysse despite her white eyes.

"Lord Varanas, he has come to Oskir and found it empty," Hjorda said. "He is angry, very angry. He will not loot it; silver and gold are nothing to him. He has decided, after much thinking, not to burn the city. His only goal is to eradicate the humans... to kill us or make us slaves. One of his servants has suggested we are going to the Drawbridge. I do not know if he will listen. Another servant argues... says White Wolves have come down from the mountains, and that they are near the Drawbridge... near *us*..."

"Stay calm," Alysse said. "We will continue on." But the thought of White Wolves—ferocious beasts only the mightiest warrior had a hope of slaying—made her queasy. "Now hurry! We will reach the King's Drawbridge tonight, or die trying." The second possibility had begun to seem likely.

Alysse quickened her pace.

"King's Drawbridge—Ten miles." The signpost was of no consolation. Night had fallen. Blinding snow flurries further obscured her vision. The shivering of the crowd, the chattering of teeth, was the only sound beside a low moaning wind.

Then a new sound echoed through the shrub-land, loud and instantly recognizable: The high-pitched, resonant howl of a White Wolf. It confirmed Alysse's worst fears, that a pack was on the hunt.

A woman screamed. A man half-drew his sword, then slid it back. An infant began to cry.

The very thought of motherhood at a time like this made Alysse shiver. "Stay calm!" she shouted. "We will face what comes in the Badelgard way: with strength, bravery, and honor!"

Their journey continued a while without struggle, and eventually even the howl of the White Wolf was forgotten. In darkness, using only the road markers as a guide, Alysse continued on. She rested her hand on the hilt of Logrin's sword. If the time came to draw it, she would. If the time came to put all the concerns of this world aside, to charge into the hordes of the enemy and meet her end, then—by the gods—she would.

"My queen!" Hjorda shouted, breaking the long silence. "Lord Varanas has set along the road. He has, at last, decided to pursue us."

"Then we must hurry!" For a moment, Alysse wondered if she took counsel from a lunatic. If Hjorda was not truly a witch, only stark, raving mad. But in a time like this, she had no choice but to trust. "We are not far from the Drawbridge!"

For a brief moment the clouds shifted, allowing the moon a brief time to shine. A signpost lay ahead: "King's Drawbridge—Three miles." The area had grown rocky and barren, covered in moss and heathland, bereft of trees. No human help would find them here; no crop could grow in this soil, and no animals could pasture here. There would be no villages, no warriors to assist them, if—indeed—there were any other humans left at all.

Hjorda whimpered louder than she ever had.

"What is it?" Alysse turned around. She could not make out the blind, mad witch among the dark shapes of the crowd.

"I have failed you, my queen... It is not my fault. I never knew."

"*What?*"

"If we go to the King's Drawbridge we will find death or bondage!" Hjorda answered. "The guardians have been slain. In their place, the Fell Lord Xenari blocks our escape. We must turn around, but Varanas is at our heels."

"Then we must face the Fell Lord." Nausea filled Alysse. "We must drive him off the Sky Cliffs."

"You are brave, my queen, but facing a Fell Lord is most unwise!" Hjorda shouted. "No human alive could slay one. They are gods of battle, impossible to overcome... unable to die because they do not live."

"Then we will die trying." A few in the crowd groaned. But what other option did Alysse have? If this other 'Fell Lord,' Varanas, pursued them along the road, they had no choice, no other option but surprise.

"If you must choose," Hjorda shouted above the crowd, "face Varanas. Killing him will be impossible. But even with his war-band, he is less a threat than Xenari. Varanas is a god of war, but Xenari is even more ancient, even more powerful. They place Xenari at the King's Drawbridge for a reason: so that none may escape."

"I don't know whether you speak the truth," Alysse said. "I don't know whether you are really a witch. But going back into the west—no matter the wisdom you possess—is foolish. We will face Xenari, god of battle or not. We will force our way onto the King's Drawbridge, because that is our only chance."

"Then you are a fool!" Hjorda snapped. "But I will follow my queen, even unto death."

The wind picked up and the night seemed to darken even further. Alysse could no longer see the road markers, only brush up against them and correct her path.

Her stomach growled. It was well past time to eat, and they had salvaged every bit of food in Oskir, but—despite her hunger—she could not waste any time to stop. If the blind witch spoke truth, an Ulfr war-band pursued them and a champion of death awaited them at the King's Drawbridge. Perhaps Hjorda was correct: they walked to their end, but if so, it would be an honorable end.

In the night, time became unclear. Several times, Alysse thought their arrival was imminent; but their stagger through darkness kept on with disappointing longevity.

A new sound echoed over the barren land, at first faint but quickly growing louder: the gallop of a warhorse along the road. For a moment, Alysse held hope that a human warrior came to aid them; she

turned, and looked back and—as the moon peeked out of the clouds—
she realized how wrong she was.

The massive black charger huffed as it tore down the road.
Sitting on it was a creature of enormous size; if a man, the largest of all
humankind. Completely covered in steel armor, two red eyes gleamed
from inside his greathelm and revealed his otherworldly nature. A Fell
Lord, most definitely; and likely Varanas. The blind witch was right.

He had caught up with them before they reached the King's
Drawbridge. Alysse swept Logrin's longsword out of its sheath. "For
Badelgard!" she cried, dug her heels into her horse's side, and charged.

She galloped along the side of the road to avoid the crowd. Some
of the men drew their own weapons as she rushed past them. She rode
to her death; she could not match even a human warrior's skill. But she
would meet an honorable end. She would serve as an example to her
people, and perhaps they would die in honor too.

In the darkness, through a veil of snow, glints of blue caught her
eye. A howl pierced through the air, and a pack of White Wolves sprinted
through the snow, revealing themselves.

A few in the crowd screamed, but by now they had all brandished
their swords and axes. Alysse had roused them to battle. But in the
middle of her charge she yanked the reigns and halted.

The Fell Lord had stopped too, waiting like a statue of iron the
gloom.

She had to weigh her options. She knew as much about the
White Wolves as anyone else. They rarely left the mountains, and when
they did, they limited themselves to the uplands of Frostfall. Seeing them
this far south made no sense. But of all the gods' creations, White
Wolves were the most territorial, and the most vicious when threatened.
Perhaps the alpha of this pack had expanded the territory to all of
Badelgard. Or perhaps something in the mountains had driven them out.

As the beasts made their first movements, it became clear the
humans were not their quarry. Step by step, they approached Varanas,
and as they drew closer to the steel-helmed titan, their growling grew

louder, angrier.

Perhaps, the White Wolves were their friends. At the least, they were not enemies.

The Fell Lord dismounted. The sound of his iron feet echoed across the snow. He drew a pale blade, immense in size, and took his first heavy trudges forward.

It was time for her to decide: *Do I run while he is distracted, or do I help these wolves?*

The Fell Lord left the road and tramped out into the open moss-land to face his canine foes. Their growling was now louder than the wind and—to Alysse—ominous.

"Turn back!" Alysse commanded. "Let us hope these noble beasts accomplish their task. And let us honor the Wolf forevermore, and make him the symbol of our fight."

After some confused scrambling of foot and hoof, the crowd turned around and headed the other way. Alysse rode forward and again assumed the vanguard which—she promised herself—would be her position from then on.

CHAPTER TWO

It was pitch-dark. The crowd marching behind her huffed in exhaustion. Alysse's back ached from riding all day and night in the saddle.

"We must rest. The night is dark, but we must rest," she said. "Fill your stomachs, and sleep a while. We are not strong like the dead; we need to rest."

"A good time." The blind witch's voice pierced the darkness. "Varanas is wounded. He killed many White Wolves, but the alpha's jaws sank deep. The pack has fled in defeat, but Varanas will not pursue us tonight."

Alysse dismounted.

She filled her stomach with road bread. A supper not fitting for a queen, she mused, but she would suffer with her people. She laid out her bedroll, got in, and within seconds drifted to sleep.

The morning light surprised her when she awoke. She thought the night would never end. She thought the snow and darkness would continue until the end of the world, until the end of time. But here it was: the sun, shining brightly through a veil of cloud, illuminating the glittering white snow and the open land that surrounded them.

In the confusion of the night, Alysse had led them along a different road. This would take them through a southern route, through Trowfell Keep and eventually descending into Andarr's Port.

Andarr's Port. What had become of it? The city where she spent her married years. The largest town in Badelgard, larger than even the king's own town. The darklings overran it, slaughtered its people. Harald was a darkling, now. Harald...

She shivered.

"My lady Alysse." The light of day shone on the witch's face. "Varanas is once again on the road. His wounds are mended now."

Alysse wrapped her winter cloak tighter. "We will keep going. The King's Drawbridge is no longer available. That leaves one exit: the sea."

"If they blocked the King's Drawbridge, then certainly they've blocked the port also!" a young woman said.

She was right, of course.

"Andarr's Port is full of darklings," a man added. "It's a house of the dead, now, or so I've been told."

"There is no other way," Alysse said. "If we perish there, we have no choice."

The road continued for a while through the open land. A pine forest lay a few hundred yards to the west.

Who knows how long it will go on?

Perhaps the road would never end.

They passed into the pine forest. Traces of life remained there: animal tracks, deer droppings. Tokens that reminded Alysse that not everything in Badelgard was dead.

In late morning, the pounding of hooves echoed through the forest. If it was Ulfr, she would face them. The winter was sapping her strength, her will. But still, she would die in honor.

They were not Ulfr: a hundred men, all human, girt in steel armor. Some bore lances. All of them wielded swords. They were Zarube knights. A standard flapped in the wind, upheld by a squire: the Red Hawk of the Voraignes shone in the light. Her army had turned against her, but if they captured her, could they be any worse lieges than the Ulfr?

Riding at the front was a man Alysse vaguely recognized. He grasped his helmet in his steel gauntlets, revealing a head of thin black hair and chestnut eyes. A fresh cut streaked across his high cheekbones.

As he thundered forward on his charge, she remembered his name: Sir Lirac. A formidable knight, young and—by all accounts—brave. His sword was drawn.

He stopped before Alysse and waved for his men to do the same. He spoke in Zarube: "Alysse. I am surprised. I was expecting another Ulfr war-band. My sword is thirsty for their blood."

"I expected Ulfr too," Alysse answered. "I am surprised but I am not sure if it will be pleasant. Sir Logrin revealed his monstrous heart after I accepted his aid. I wonder if your heart is monstrous as well."

"You are my lady," Sir Lirac said. "I will protect your life at the expense of my own. The land of Badelgard is dark and dangerous. I will protect you and your people as best I can."

Warmth flooded through Alysse; the ice within her, for a second, thawed. She wanted to embrace Sir Lirac. She did not. Instead, she had to know. "How are things? Where are the others?"

Lirac frowned. "The answers to both your questions are grave, I'm afraid. For a while I rode with Sir Carbidonne and his party. He has fallen." He slid his sword back into its sheath, and the others followed. He bowed his head. "We set upon an Ulfr caravan. We killed scores of them but there was one we could not defeat: an iron giant, a man of steel."

"A Fell Lord," Alysse said.

"I ordered a retreat when the battle turned grim. The—" He peered into Alysse's eyes. "—the Fell Lord… he buried Sir Carbidonne in a length of steel. His men would not leave his side, not even at the threshold of death. I am sure they perished as well."

Alysse touched her chest, feeling weak. "I am sorry for him. You must feel guilty for retreating…"

"I am ashamed."

"But you should not be! You are alive and strong." She smiled. "You have come in our darkest hour. In the end, your swords may not deliver us, but I'm sure I speak for all my people when I say that your presence comforts our hearts."

For the first time Alysse remembered, Lirac smiled. "I am pleased to serve you, milady. I will accompany you wherever you go, and fight in your name."

"Then you are a better man, already, than Logrin ever was."

They rode hard through the day. Alysse rode at the vanguard, as she promised herself, alongside Sir Lirac.

At noon, a village appeared along the road. The thatch roofs of the longhouses shone gold in the sunlight. In the central square, however, a mass of darklings jabbered to themselves. If these creatures had a language, Alysse guessed it could only communicate the most basic of thoughts: *kill* or *eat*.

"Should we avoid them?" Alysse said.

"No," Lirac answered. "These are the weakest of the dead, as mortal as the living." He drew his sword and galloped forward. His men followed quickly after and—in the span of a moment—fell upon the darklings.

With the darklings cut down, the village lay empty. The knights forward out to scout out the area while the refugees entered the homes, starved for good food. As Alysse expected, they were disappointed; the small amount of food that remained was spoiled. One man, undeterred, had his fill of moldy bread before spitting it out into the snow.

Through all the commotion, Alysse could not help but gaze at the blind witch. She was muttering against the wind, an outcast among outcasts. She had made an evil decision earlier in her life, but she had—by all accounts—changed her ways.

As the crowd salvaged everything they could find from the abandoned homes, Alysse turned her horse gently around, and rode up to the witch.

Hjorda looked up at her queen. Alysse sensed, despite the lack of detail in her eyes, that this witch was afraid. "Hello, Hjorda," Alysse said. "Is there something wrong?"

"Varanas is coming." She grasped one of her bone amulets. "Angry that you've escaped... but above all, he is angry with *me*."

"Sir Lirac is a good man," Alysse said. "He will not let you die. Moreover, I will not let you die. You have made a mistake in your life, but I forgive you on behalf of Badelgard. You are one of my people, and I will defend you like the others."

"Thank you!" Hjorda sounded hysterical. "So few good people in this world... so few, so few." Like clockwork, her lips began to tremble again. "Lord Varanas was in my dream last night. He said 'You sold your soul to the Great Mother. If you abandon her, you owe her your life.' He said he will hang me from a tree... make a cup out of my skull."

Alysse shivered. "I will not let him touch you."

"You have much less power than you think." Hjorda backed away, hands trembling. "We must go... we must go at once. Lord Varanas has found our route. He has alerted the other Fell Lords. One has taken control of Trowfell Keep. The earl's wife Carolyn has been tossed from the parapets. It has become a market for human slaves. The poor victims, bound in chains, sent all over Badelgard to serve under witches and—"

"Enough!" Alysse shouted. "We will go now. But where will we go? That is a far more difficult decision! But we will go!"

"We should not have killed the darklings." Hjorda continued talking, despite Alysse's demands. "A witch created them from the slain villagers... they are her children, and she knows when they are gone. We must hurry. Gods! We must hurry before I am hung from a tree, and a chalice is made from my skull!"

"Silence!" Alysse screamed. But nonetheless she heeded the advice. Her heart thundered in her chest as she rode around the village, demanding that everyone drop what they carry and leave at once.

They hastened across the road. The thought of the coming night sickened Alysse; somehow she knew it would be darker and deadlier than the last. Perhaps she would never see another dawn.

Alysse saw death in the shadows of the trees. What lurked there? The witch who gave the dead villagers false life... she surely pursued them now. What was she? Who was she? A lady of high birth, surely; but a dark lady, cold and cunning, as heartless as she was beautiful. And with her rode her mate, a Fell Lord bearing the standard of the Frozen Skull.

The sun grew low, imperceptibly but inevitably, and as the light faded so did Alysse's hope. The forest continued, and darkness settled among the boughs of the pines. Just as night fell, when the sun had completed its long journey, Hjorda spoke. Her voice, not especially loud, stood out against the silence: "They're here."

Sir Lirac had placed half his men at the vanguard, and half at the rear. Regardless of where they came from, the Ulfr would meet stiff resistance.

Soon the direction became clear: from the west, the light of a lantern gleamed in the distance. "Shall we charge?" Alysse said.

"Wait," Lirac answered. "There's something strange..."

"What is it?" she said, but did not receive an answer. She bit her lip and waited it out, as they drew nearer and more torches appeared over the crest of a hill.

There were men on horses, dressed in the steel full-plate of Zarube knights. But their standards, flapping in the wind, did not bear the Red Hawk of the Voraignes, but instead the Frozen Skull of the Ulfr kingdom. A woman walked at the front, clearly one of the Ulfr. Her hair, black as jet, fell in twin braids along her shoulders. She gazed at Alysse, and her clear yellow eyes seemed to command her: *"Swear fealty to me."*

"Sir Cherbot!" Lirac cried. "Have you lost your mind?"

Only then did Alysse spot the fat knight riding in on his charger. He looked up and gazed at his former brother-in-arms, but all soul seemed to have left his eyes. "Lirac!" he grunted. "I have not lost my mind. The Ulfr have won. There is no way out. There is no exit. I have a new lady now, and I will fight in her name."

Lirac answered with a shout. "So you have abandoned Jacouette... betrayed your wife and wed yourself to a witch. I thought you fought in Jacouette's name alone."

They were now within several yards. Alysse ordered them to stop.

Cherbot drew his sword. "There is no exit. There is no way out. I serve Lady Mara now. I am her champion. I slew the people of Garn's Rock in her name. If you stand in my way, I will do the same to you."

Despite the heated conversation, the dark lady remained silent, her hand unmoving as it grasped her wooden staff. Behind her yellow eyes' apparent lack of depth, Alysse knew the witch was calculating something.

"So it was you that slew the people in the village," Lirac replied. "I knew you were lazy. I knew you preferred fish jellies and duck livers to the art of the sword. But I didn't think it would come to this."

"Here are my terms!" The witch's shrill voice, when at last it came, forced all others into silence. "You will lay down your arms. You will submit to the Great Witch, Enara, and all of you—highborn and low—will become serfs under me. In return, I will spare your lives." She bent her staff forward. "If you try to resist, you will be immediately and unconditionally destroyed."

Glints of blue flickered in the distance. White Wolves.

"Mara... that is your name, correct?"

The witch did not respond, as Alysse expected.

"You wish us to surrender to you unconditionally... to call your queen our ruler, and—presumably—to call your goddess our own. If we are serfs, where will we serve?"

"That is of no concern to you," she answered. "Do you accept the terms?"

"I'm simply curious. Where will we serve?"

"Enough. You are testing my patience." The witch glanced into the forest, perhaps sensing the wolves.

Alysse, on pure whim, slammed her heels into her horse's side and clucked. Immediately the beast took off at a breakneck gallop. In mid-stride, Alysse drew her sword. By the time the witch looked back, she was upon her, and swung her best blow.

It nicked the witch's wrinkled cheek and slashed through the cloth of her robe. Her horse bucked onto its hind legs and Alysse fell hard into the snow. A crack resounded; a sharp pain as something split and broke. She staggered to her feet regardless.

Sir Lirac and his men had just begun their gallop.

"Kill her!" the witch hissed, and Cherbot positioned himself to do just that.

The White Wolves sprinted out of the darkness just as the ranks of knights collided. The witch dodged a blow from one of the knights, but Alysse—filled with a rage she never thought she possessed—tackled the witch to the ground. She raked her nails across the witch's face, kneed her hard. She spit into her eyes and smothered her with her palms. The pent-up rage toward the Ulfr, these destroyers of life, strengthened each of her blows. Even as the witch worked magic and Alysse felt the wilting power drain her and add years to her age, she kept striking. At last she drew blood, but it wasn't enough. It wouldn't be enough until she tore the witch to piecemeal, until the only thing left of her was her evil spirit.

At some point in the frenzy, she stood up and screamed, heaving the sword to the side and then—just as quickly—swung it back, severing the witch's head. It wasn't enough; she continued slashing well beyond the point of death, until at last she realized the battle around her was over, and the knights of Zarubain and the refugees of Badelgard were staring at her in disbelief.

"You are vicious, milady," Lirac said.

Alysse looked at the black blood staining her cloak, and flushed hot in embarrassment.

"A warrior queen, you are," Lirac continued, "a woman of battle, braver than most men I know. I revere you, milady, and I will serve you with my life."

Alysse smiled, but still, her rage simmered. Her longsword dripped with blood. The refugees knelt before her.

"Never before," a man said, "has there been a better ruler of Badelgard. I agree with the southlander… I will serve you with my life, and follow you to the gates of Hell."

Andarr's Port, he meant.

CHAPTER THREE

Despite the victory, the night held more dangers. The White Wolves remained. A few began to eat, pawing off the dead Zarubes' armor and burying themselves muzzle-deep in their flesh. The alpha—largest of the pack—gazed at Alysse with his glittering blue eyes. His coat was as white as the snow, a pure unblemished color. His fangs, sharp and yellow, gleamed as he saluted the moon and let out an icy howl.

White Wolves, wild and vicious though they were… hunters of those who ventured into the mountain passes… they were not, truly, the enemies of humanity. They hated the Ulfr like Alysse did. Yet despite their alliance, Alysse could not thank the alpha or speak with him. Instead, she sheathed her bloody sword, and knelt before him.

Again, the alpha saluted the moon and let out a howl. A few other wolves followed their lord. The alpha then turned his head, gazing into the darkness and perhaps seeing something Alysse did not see. The wolves who were eating stopped, looking up at their lord the alpha, muzzles covered in blood and gristle.

Then, as soon as they had come, the pack was gone, vanishing into the darkness. "I salute you!" Alysse called after them, and the alpha answered with a bark.

Sir Lirac appeared before her, trotting out of the darkness. "Strange times we live in, when wolves are our friends."

"Perhaps, they have always been our friends, and we never knew," Alysse said. She looked down at what remained of the witch's corpse—hacked, slashed, and shredded—and shivered at her own handiwork. Then she mounted her horse. Blood soaked her dress. "Let's go. Perhaps we should stay off the road… but how, then, would we find Andarr's Port?"

"Varanas will find us regardless." The witch's voice rose above the wind and the noises of the crowd.

"Then let us continue," Alysse ordered, and their trek began again.

The darkness deepened. Again, Alysse wondered if the night would ever end. The light of day—the sun—seemed to have last touched them eons ago.

At some point in this eternity of darkness and cold, lights appeared on a hill. Numerous lights: a city. Trowfell Keep, yet in this fell winter, Alysse knew things were not as they had been. Carolyn Trowfell—proud, noble woman that she was—tossed from a high wall by the Ulfr... or so the witch had said.

At the sight of the city lights, the witch shouted: "Trowfell Keep is now a market for human slaves! The scions of the House Trowfell have been put to death. It is a home of evil spirits, a house of darkness... the Fell Lord Galcani rules over it. He has surely felt the death of Lady Mara; she ruled with him."

"And what shall we do, then?" Alysse said.

"There is nothing to do," the witch answered. "He has sent a war-band to destroy us. Varanas is not far behind. We are surrounded; the best we can hope for is an easy death. Galcani will not forgive us for Mara's death. The Ulfr have won the war... we should surrender."

"Quiet!" Alysse snarled. "We will not surrender. If you speak such evil words again, I will burn you according to the Badelgard way. Understood?"

The witch did not answer.

"Off road!" Alysse shouted. "We go north, and see where the night takes us!"

"Come!" Lirac answered. "You heard the lady. Into the wilds, and to the end of all things, we will follow her."

The snow had deepened. The horse's knees barely reached above. Shrill winds had begun to blow out of the north, as if to hamper them. But if an Ulfr witch had conjured it up to halt their advance, she would be disappointed. Their trek would continue.

"Lord Varanas has joined with the war-band!" Alysse had grown to hate the blind witch's voice. "They are following our tracks now. It is only a matter of time before they slay us all, and forever we will lie in an icy tomb."

"Another word," Alysse shrieked, "and I will have Sir Lirac chop off your head. But I would guess, even then, you'd blabber on. You have been warned, Hjorda. And that is your last warning."

"Yes, Your Majesty," she answered.

Eventually, the lights of Trowfell Keep vanished into the darkness and snow. Even against the wind, the chattering of teeth rose above. Despite their heavy clothing, some began to succumb to the cold. If the Ulfr failed to accomplish their goal, perhaps the winter would claim them.

The night would never end... Alysse was certain of that, now. Eternal darkness, eternal winter, and once the Fell Lord had buried his blade in her chest, she would rise again as a creature of darkness. As a dark lady, a siren, a queen of the dead, singing her mournful song to whoever would hear her: *they claimed my life, and gave me a false one.*

Sir Lirac grasped her hand. Even through the gloves she wore, she felt his warmth, his spirit. In a better time, in a better place, perhaps they could have loved each other. But the time was dark and the place was fell. Death hovered above them, ready to take their souls; yet their souls would not go with Him. Their souls would remain in their bodies, twisted into dark, wicked shades, and Alysse and Sir Lirac would wander Badelgard as darklings or hungry revenants.

His grip tightened. In her mind she protested; it was not the right time, or the right place. Their doom was nigh. She wriggled out of his grasp.

"I am sorry, milady," Sir Lirac said.

Alysse groaned. "Do not be sorry... you are a good man. But the time is dark, and the end is close-by. In another age, in another place, in the light of the sun, then perhaps..."

The winds died down. The darkness continued. Snow fell silently in thick flakes. The clouds had obscured the moon for hours. Alysse had no idea what time it was, but she knew the Fell Lord pursued them at some distance, or perhaps at their heels. In total darkness the land began to drop; they had begun to descend into the river valley.

In the west, a red spark glimmered over the horizon. But Alysse had been through this night long enough, had been through this winter long enough, to know that hope was futile. Dawn would never come again; daylight would never come again. The sun had left, and would never shine on the world again.

But eventually, she could no longer deny it. The sun was rising, red as blood. Light gleamed over the snowy boughs of the pines. Alysse wanted to sleep, but she could not.

She looked back in the new light, noticing a few were gone. The winter had claimed some, and now their bodies would lay frozen for eternity. A better fate, Alysse knew, than a fell wound and a new, false life. That fate awaited her.

"Stop!" she shouted. "Stop, and eat. Rest a while."

The valley descended many miles to the river, frozen as it gushed from King's Falls so far away. The Fell Lord was certainly close. But at some point, they had to rest. They had to eat. They were not strong, like the dead; they needed rest.

In the light of the morning, they ate the last bits of food that remained: scraps of biscuits, and—for the lucky—the last morsels of smoked salmon and salted meat. Alysse resolved to only eat biscuits; if she led her people, she had to suffer with the least among them—a philosophy King Sven had never believed.

By the time she finished her meager fare, she was still hungry. More pressingly, her eyes drooped; she wanted sleep more than anything else, but she would have to continue the trek despite her increasing delirium. If she stopped here, they would have no chance of escape... if, even, they had any chance at all.

A noise woke her from her thoughts: a shrill scream. She turned, looking up the side of the valley, and saw the blind witch Hjorda, writhing in the snow. Despite her exhaustion, Alysse climbed the slope as Hjorda's screams continued.

"Hjorda!" Alysse's voice was hoarse. "What is wrong?"

"She has claimed me... She has claimed me... I am Her slave. Her evil eye is upon us."

"Who?"

"The Great Mother... Her throne is nearly pulled from the ice. Her icy hand... I cannot breathe." She gasped.

"If only we had a priestess with us," Alysse said. "Perhaps we should have gone to the temple in Vanaheim." The priestesses knew the healing arts. But they had gone too far past it... crossed the White River, frozen solid, without realizing it. The snow cover had been so deep, the night, so dark that human senses failed them.

"Varanas has called off the pursuit," Hjorda said. "He doesn't think you're a threat. He knows there is no escape... that Andarr's Port is a hive of darklings and undead, and that Xenari blocks the drawbridge. He knows that either the winter or another Fell Lord will destroy you." Despite her eyes' lack of detail, her blind gaze seemed to grow more intense. "I am no longer an asset to you. You must kill me, my queen... the Great Mother is so close to incarnation, she can see through me. She will know where I am, where *you* are. Kill me."

"Never," Alysse said. "I will not kill one of my own people unless they have committed a crime."

"I have committed a crime," Hjorda said, "a crime worthy of death. I have pledged myself to the Great Mother in exchange for power. I have struggled to break free, to right my wrongs. But I cannot be forgiven."

"I forgive you."

"Kill me."

"No," Alysse said as firmly as she could. "I will not."

Hjorda removed her small leather pack. She pulled out a wooden bowl and discarded it in the snow. She grabbed a spoon of horn, and discarded that as well. Then she produced a small knife, and before Alysse realized her intent, Hjorda had slashed her wrists. A stream of red snaked from her hands through the snow.

Alysse screamed. "No! I told you, *no.*" She fell onto Hjorda, grabbed her hands but realized there was nothing to be done. There was no healer skillful enough to bind these wounds.

Around the hill, the refugees stared at the dying woman—some in disbelief or shock, but none in concern. She had been an outsider in life, and she was an outsider in death.

Alysse stood up, seeing that her gloves dripped red. Tears welled in her eyes. She had seen enough death for a lifetime. She had seen enough cruelty, enough blood-thirst. The Ulfr and their Great Mother had received their payment. Hjorda had lost her life, despite Alysse's best efforts.

A hand grasped Alysse's glove. She turned; Sir Lirac stood beside her. "I am sorry, milady," he said. His chestnut eyes—though they, too had seen much death—still retained a childlike warmth. "I am sorry it happened. But whatever your course of action, do not blame yourself."

"There is no escape." Alysse wiped her eyes. "She confirmed my fears. Andarr's Port crawls with darklings. Whatever course of action I take, I am sure it will spell our end."

"Then let it be a glorious end," Lirac said. He smiled. "We will charge into the ranks of the enemy and surely perish. But we will die fighting the Ulfr."

"Yes. Yes, we will die in a glorious charge." Alysse smiled. "But first, we must sleep."

CHAPTER FOUR

Alysse laid out her bedroll. They had no tents, not even for a queen. She would sleep a few hours, at most, and then they would continue to Andarr's Port. In sight of Riverhall Castle, they would charge into the darkling ranks and surely perish.

Sir Lirac was not resting. He was mounting his charger, perhaps riding off to scout the area. A man of steel, a man of war, but a good man...

Alysse slept a short time. When she woke, she was still tired, and a bit famished, but she had to set an example.

And despite the brightness of day, and the sun—now peeking through the clouds—she knew very well what lay all around her. The dead did not perish in the sun like they used to. They walked in broad daylight like the living, now, in spite of all the legends. In midnight tales, the storytellers said the dead perished in the light of the sun. If it was ever true, it was not true anymore.

She stood up, and as the weight shifted back to her legs, the extent of her exhaustion hit her. She looked around, saw the refugees— some half-sleeping, some wide awake—and began to pack for the journey ahead of them. They would reach Andarr's Port by nightfall. There, they would make their last stand.

The thundering of hooves echoed from higher up the slope. Sir Lirac, handsome and girt in heavy steel, was riding toward her with his fellow warriors. He halted a few yards away from her, and the others followed. "Milady," he said.

Alysse curtsied.

"I'm not sure we should attack Andarr's Port."

"Why not?"

"I scouted the area. An Ulfr caravan goes west to Oskir from Trowfell Keep. Their cargo: human slaves. They are intended as religious sacrifices to the Ulfr goddess."

"And how do you know this, Sir Lirac?"

Lirac glanced back. One of the other knights tossed a large object into the snow. Only after careful examination did she realize it was a body: an Ulfr man, his beard torn off, and his body cut to the point of disfigurement.

"We captured their scout. He told us everything, after a bit of persuasion."

"Whatever he went through," Alysse said, "he deserved ten more lifetimes of it. Although, Sir Lirac, I must warn you. The Ulfr do not think like us. I'm not altogether certain that the information is accurate."

"I am sure, milady," he said. "Under the knife or the stretcher or the thumbscrew, truth pours out of the vilest blackguard."

Alysse pursed her lips. The disfiguring of the corpse—despite its Ulfr nature—sickened her. She decided not to ever look at it again. "Sir Lirac, you are a wise man. You have seen much in your time. I am sure my father, and Sir Jourmande, sent you into war countless times. If your conviction is absolute, then I trust your judgment. We will assault the caravan."

Sir Lirac smiled. "A wise choice, milady. Perishing in a glorious charge is well and good; but victory is better."

"The refugees will stay behind. Leave a few men to guard them. The rest will attack. And I will ride with you."

"I would tell you no, but I don't think you would listen." Sir Lirac's smile grew wider. "There is no armor for you. Several of my men have passed on, but their bodies and their armor lie many miles away."

"I will ride with you anyway."

It was noon when they departed. Open fields lay all around them, and the snow glittered in the sunlight.

A woman riding into battle on a charger. Her father would never believe it. The whole of Zarubain would not believe it. In Badelgard, they had legends of valkyries, of battle-maidens that served the goddess Vana. To her adopted people, it might not seem as strange. But in Zarubain, place of her birth, no such legends existed. Her father would not believe it, but then again, her father would never talk to her again. Her ambition had, perhaps, taken her too far. She had been too trusting of Jourmande, too naïve to think those knights would serve in her name. If her father would hear it, she would apologize for her wrongs; but he would not, and moreover, she would not live to tell him.

As they rode across the open fields, through the thick snow, she looked at Sir Lirac. His helmet lay in his hand, revealing his short, dark hair. Few men of war had such a noble heart, or so it seemed. And though he was not handsome like her husband Harald, she could only feel her draw to him strengthening. In another time, in another place, perhaps she could have remarried. He could have been her support through the dark times, but not in this life.

Her husband now wandered the land as a darkling. Her baby had gone to the grave, to the realm of the dead. Her twins—the ones that had survived—had become priests of the Green Dragon. They had left to fight trolls. Ha! She had not believed it, at first, but now she saw it for herself. The world was coming undone. Things out of dark legend walked in the full light of day. And if the priests of the Green Dragon had met trolls on the Ice Shelf, then gods help them. They would need divine aid to overcome the Ulfr. And the gods, on the whole, seemed to have abandoned Badelgard altogether.

She looked at Sir Lirac, riding through the snow. In another time, in another place.

"There!" Lirac roared.

In the distance, a dark haze of silhouettes appeared. It was time. Alysse drew her sword, rimmed with dried blood. She would make her stand. She was no warrior; she had no training with the blade. But she would fight with Sir Lirac and the others, and perish.

It was how she wanted to leave the mortal world: at the front of a charge, overcoming the mortal concerns of death and life, sacrificing herself for a cause. Better than dying in slavery to the Ulfr on a premature deathbed, with the full weight of her cowardice upon her.

The haze of silhouettes eventually took on a clearer shape. Thirty humans—mostly men, but a few women—bound in iron ball and chain. No Ulfr guarded them. They were struggling to move, but could only pull themselves an inch or so at a time, and with great strain to their legs. A few dozen yards away, a small pine forest grew. Could their Ulfr lords be waiting there? It was possible.

The other possibility came to her quickly thereafter. In the darkness of the forest, some branches cracked underfoot. A group of Ulfr appeared out of the gloom.

She looked behind her. More Ulfr, surrounding them in a ring. It was a trap. A trap she thought they could overcome, until the Fell Lord came tramping out of the forest gloom. His red eyes smoldered from behind the black helmet. His sword, like the rest of his kind, shone pale white, and even from a distance Alysse sensed its chill.

"Charge?" Alysse did not intend it as a question, but sometimes she surprised herself.

"No," Sir Lirac answered. "We will wait…"

His voice trailed off. Alysse never pictured a situation where fear would rule Sir Lirac. But the sight of the Fell Lord—the plates of his steel armor covered in mournful faces, and those red coals of eyes— made it all understandable.

Alysse's arm ached at the weight of the sword. "Sir Lirac? I thought we would perish in a glorious charge—"

"It all seems glorious in idle talk." His voice quivered. "But a knight must be wise. He must…"

Again his voice trailed off. Alysse gulped and looked around. The Ulfr completely encircled them. In the far distance, the smoldering red eyes of another Fell Lord appeared. Perhaps one of these called himself Varanas. But names did not matter; the Ulfr host drew closer.

"Charge!" Alysse demanded, but neither Sir Lirac nor his men obeyed. Her horse bucked up and whinnied. She would not charge alone.

At least, not yet.

Closer and closer the Ulfr marched. Before Alysse knew it, they were within yards. They stopped, surrounded by a sea of Ulfr that stretched into the distance without end. Nausea seized her. Sir Lirac's face had gone white; his sword-arm trembled. One man backed away, only for an Ulfr poll-axe to prod him.

The human lure, bound in shackles, were not trembling like Sir Lirac and his men. They stood calmly. But in reality, these sons and daughters of Badelgard had simply given up—or so it seemed to Alysse.

The Ulfr men surrounded them, many ranks deep. Thick hair covered their coarse, hide-like skin. Their black and brown beards fell to their knees. If they had any relation to humans, they were mockeries of their cousins like the wildmen of legend. Their pointed ears indicated an Elvish heritage, but even that comparison seemed inaccurate. Alysse had seen only a few elves in her life, but the ones she did see were graceful, slender, and not nearly as hairy.

The ranks of the Ulfr parted and the Fell Lord marched ahead. His heavy iron footsteps echoed through the air. A voice like an infernal choir spoke through the helmet: "Greetings. I am Lord Varanas. And you are Alysse, who claims to be queen of Sorelda."

"Sorelda, you call it." Alysse's voice did not tremble as she expected. "The land is properly called Badelgard, and I am queen of that."

The Fell Lord gazed at Alysse, saying nothing for a while. She could only meet those smoldering red eyes a half-second before she had to look away.

"What are your terms?" Sir Lirac's voice did tremble. "I wish to be reasonable. I think we can come to an agreement without violence."

"Without violence, you say," the Fell Lord boomed. "I am not sure."

"What do you want?" Sir Lirac said. "If it is in my power I will give it."

"Lirac!" Alysse hissed. Perhaps he was not the man she thought.

"What do I want?" the Fell Lord said in his many-stranded voice. "A few days ago, I would have wanted unconditional surrender. That does not satisfy me any longer. You refused our initial terms. You killed Lady Mara. You have already proven yourself obstinate and impossible to govern. If I allowed you a life of slavery, you would plot ways to escape."

"I would not!" Lirac said.

The Fell Lord, twice the size of Lirac even on his horse, strode even closer. A shaking consumed Lirac's entire body. The other men backed away, but they were surrounded.

Alysse's arm burned. The sword was heavy, but held it high.

"I surrender unconditionally," Lirac said. "I will serve the Great Mother as my goddess, and abandon my worship of Marabelle. I swear fealty to your queen."

"Too late." The Fell Lord grasped his sword tighter. "We cannot have an armed force wreaking havoc on Sorelda. Mara gave you our terms; you refused them, and killed her."

"*She* killed Mara!" Lirac's iron-lined finger pointed at Alysse.

She gasped, but had no breath. It was time. Sir Lirac was not the knight she believed, the one she thought she could love. No. *It's time.*

The Fell Lord's blade came whistling down. Lirac thrust his upward in an attempt to parry; his steel blade shattered in two against the strange white metal. Another swing, and the Fell Lord cleaved him in half.

The other warriors scattered. Some made a feeble attempt to battle the Ulfr. None of them charged with conviction. Alysse would be the only one. Her arm burned from the weight of the sword. Likely, she would fail to even land her blow. But it was time. It was time to charge.

She kicked her heels and urged her horse at a breakneck gallop. A blow from the Fell Lord's white blade grazed her hair. The line of Ulfr was before her. She prepared to land her blow. A javelin missed her. She rode to her death. She would die with conviction. She would die fighting the Ulfr.

PART THREE: DRAGON'S SON

CHAPTER ONE

Things looked so small from the sky. The pines formed a single green mass. The blood of the dragon gave him strength to fight the Ulfr, and wings to fly, but his vision remained human. Now, flapping his newfound wings with Gudrun the Battle-Maiden on his back, he traveled Badelgard swifter than any Elvish horse could take him.

There was the river running down: a thin line almost imperceptible, snaking through rocky cliffs. There was the valley, its precipices becoming gentler and gentler until they became hills. As Gudrun barked orders—*Now left! Now right!*—there, nearly beyond his sight, lay Frost Lake and somewhere, Blackhelm Keep straddling its shores.

There was a glimmer of gray to his right: a haze that could only be the Ice Shelf, by now filled with trolls. And for a brief moment, he thought he heard a groan echoing, a shrill sonic scream, from somewhere in the center of the Shelf.

"They are pulling the Statue of the Great Mother out of the ice!" Gudrun cried. "The Great Witch watches as a hundred trolls wrench it from its place."

"Then let me slay them!" Kai cried.

"You are not strong enough!" Gudrun shouted.

Kai snarled louder than he thought possible, like a bear or a lion, or perhaps like a dragon.

"You will be strong enough, one day!" Gudrun said. "In time, you will scorch the trolls with fire. Now you're straying left! *Right!* Go right! Follow the river!"

"Where are we going?" Kai snarled. His voice had changed; it had become low and hoarse, yet louder.

"Before you face the Great Witch, there are things that need doing! We fly to Frostfall. In the shadow of the mountains, there is a forest of the damned. There, you must learn a lesson. You must learn—as all good leaders of men—the nature of your enemy. You must learn what drives them to do what they do, and where their evil first began."

"I can learn nothing from those savages."

"Perhaps you cannot learn anything from them; but you can learn *about* them. Besides—loath as I am to say it—these Ulfr, these mockeries of elvenkind, they consider *your people* unlearned savages. In all, they may not be wrong."

"Careful with your words," Kai roared, and felt heat course from his breath. "Else, I might buck you off my back."

"Your transformation has begun," Gudrun hollered, "but your best efforts would fail to shake a battle-maiden from her place. Our feet are like the roots of the mountains, unmovable until Lady Vana commands us to take flight."

"I would not put that to the test," Kai snarled.

The Ice Shelf continued in the distance, a faint haze of gray. The sound returned, aching in Kai's ears: a muffled, half-voiced scream from the center of the shelf. A goddess half-buried in an icy tomb, her screams nonetheless carrying for miles.

Yet as he looked at the handful of hardscrabble villages along the river, Kai sensed that the people down below could not hear the scream. The noise—if heard by the ears at all—was directed at the mind. Directed at Kai, to break him.

He shivered.

There was the Waterwood, white and frozen solid. He searched for Wildsaber Keep among the snow and failed to find it. Then, eventually, its location dawned on him: a blackened, burned-out shell on a hill, barely perceptible from so high up. But there it was: the former home of the Wildsabers, abandoned and utterly destroyed.

Far beyond was the sea and Andarr's Port. Before he drew too close, Gudrun shouted her command: "*Right! Right!* We go north to Frostfall. The army at the port is so massive they would pose a danger to even you."

"I doubt it!" Kai roared, but nonetheless he obeyed, flying over the valley as it made its ascent.

The highlands of Frostfall appeared. Despite the Ulfr invasion, Kai guessed it looked much the same. It had never been well-farmed or heavily populated. White Wolf Keep had once stood alone among rocky pastures, though its fate now—Kai guessed—was grim.

"Make your descent! Make your descent!" Gudrun cried. "We must tread this land carefully."

Kai snarled again. He never liked receiving commands, but now—in this new form, this new self—he hated it, and for a second contemplated bucking Gudrun off his back, or at least trying.

He dove down, letting the wind carry him. A green mass became a clump of forest. The clump of forest became trees.

"This isn't going to end well!"

Gudrun's ominous warning came bare seconds before Kai hit the ground. In a lesser state, he would have broken every one of his bones. But somehow his ribs resisted the impact, even as he broke through the snow, tore up through the grass and skidded through the mud. At last he hit a tree. It splintered with a loud crack, and fell over.

At some point in the descent, Gudrun had hopped off his back. He looked up at the gray sky. He was bleeding in several places. The impact stole the air from his lungs. He only wanted to lay there and not move a muscle.

And so, he did, until Gudrun's face appeared above him. "That was not very graceful, Dragon's Son."

Despite his new form, his new self, he laughed. A resonant laugh from the pit of his stomach, the kind that takes you over and, for its duration, cures all your ills.

Gudrun joined him, even falling upon him in her laughter.

Valkyries, Kai supposed, were not always sad, somber creatures. "Ah," Kai said. His eyes welled with tears. "It is good to laugh. We have arrived in Frostfall."

"So we have," said Gudrun, smiling widely. "So we have, Dragon's Son."

As they walked through the highlands of Frostfall, it became clear that—though Kai had landed in a stand of pines—trees grew rarer the deeper they traveled. The winds seemed harsher than Badelgard's lower altitudes, blowing in gusts and send up clouds of spraying white snow as Gudrun led the way northwards.

The roads were nowhere to be seen. Kai followed Gudrun, and the cold seemed to deepen despite the mostly cloudless sky. Then— when the sun hung in the middle of the sky—a low horn bellowed across the fields.

"An Ulfr horn, I presume," Kai said.

Gudrun frowned. Her gold-streaked hair flowed in the wind, complementing her helmet well. Yet the spear she held, despite her full battle-maiden gear, seemed a worthless tool against the Ulfr. "Disappointing," she finally said. "Somehow, they know we're here. I recognize the horn. Likely, some Ulfr chieftain has sent a hunting party. Prepare for battle, Kai, if we cannot evade them."

"I have no weapon."

"Your body is a weapon."

Kai gulped. Regardless of whether she spoke truth, he never felt ready for battle without a sword or axe in his hand.

"We will continue north," Gudrun said. "North to the forest of the damned, or until the Ulfr find us."

The horn bellowed again, closer this time. Kai wrung his hands, wanting—despite his newfound powers—the comfort of a leather hilt in his sword-arm.

Gudrun marched on, against the wind, taking large strides as she looked ahead in singular determination. But Kai did not have to wait long before—through a veil of windblown snow—the Ulfr hunters revealed themselves.

A sleigh, painted black, appeared just ahead. Neither horse nor dog pulled it. Instead—in a mockery of the common beasts of burden—human-like creatures carried it forward. Yoked by iron collars, these half-rotted men pulled it perhaps faster than horses could. The explanation was obvious: a thin but painful-looking metal lash bit into their skin and propelled them as the driver shouted, *"An! An!"*

Kai hardly had a chance to observe the driver before she was upon them: a woman—that much was clear—and obviously nonhuman, judging by her pointed ears, her yellow eyes, and her coarse skin. She wore a crimson dress the color of blood. Behind her, in the backseat, another Ulfr blew the horn again.

Just as the sleigh was about to make an impact—and just as Kai was about to land his first strike—the vehicle stopped, spraying snow as the fetid stench of the undead beasts-of-burden billowed over them.

"You have entered the domain of Lord Arxani and his lady Thanara." She spoke in the Badelgardic tongue, though with a strange, almost Elvish-sounding accent. "I would say you are human, and send you to the slave markets in 'Trowfell Keep,' as they call it, if it were not for your strange wings. Your partner here seems human, but you do not."

Kai said nothing. Seeing the woman's eyes, knowing of her Ulfr nature, aroused the dragon-fire of wrath within him.

"Do you speak?" the Ulfr-woman said. "Tell me, are you undead, and if so, who is your creator?"

"He is undead," Gudrun said. Her grasp on the spear tightened. "I created him. We are messengers, carrying news to a—"

"Enough deceit!" Kai roared. "That is not my way." Kai took a step back, and his wings grew rigid of their own accord, as if preparing to fly. "I would make demands on you, witch, but I desire nothing from you except to see you die."

The witch—for that, he guessed, was her profession—reached down. When her hand returned in view, it grasped a wooden staff topped with a skull-shaped gem. But already, he was rushing toward her.

"Kai!" Gudrun cried. "Fool!"

He leapt, and landed on the seat of the sleigh. He struck the horn-blower with his fist, and a loud crack indicated broken bones. The witch, by now, had her staff ready, and her trembling lips doubtlessly incanted some dark spell.

Kai felt his wings flex to their full size and harden to their full rigidity. Whether the sight of them frightened her, or whether the power of the dragon overwhelmed her, it did not matter. The staff snapped in two and the skull-gem turned a dull black color. Blue light burst from the crack and fell in glowing sparks. The witch's yellow eyes turned shallow. Panic, Kai noticed with glee, and smiled.

He leapt upon her and hesitated. Striking a woman was against his honor, against what he believed. But he reminded himself that she posed a threat to him, that she practiced the magical arts. And as her lips again began to move, and an eldritch gleam shone in her eyes, the immediacy of his danger dawned on him.

At once he began to strike her, beating her mercilessly with his fists, breaking bones and crushing her until at last, all life left her eyes. Immediately, regret overwhelmed him; killing a woman was in such opposition to his code of honor.

Even as she lay there, beaten to death, a wind arose. It was not a normal wind, sent shrieking down from the mountains. It arose from the witch's body. Kai stumbled backward. A silvery gray wisp emerged from her body, constantly shifting in shape, but at times taking the form of an ancient, wicked crone. At last it broke free of the witch's body and hissed as it flew northward: "Lady Thanara is not so easily defeated."

With the death—or temporary death—of the witch, the undead beasts-of-burden fell limp. Their iron yoke forced them upright, but nonetheless their false life had left them.

Kai took a few deep breaths. "I have seen more witchcraft in these past few days than I have in my entire life."

"Yes," Gudrun said. Her smile was joyless. "You have slain Lady Thanara, but you have underestimated her powers of necromancy. In this fell winter she will live on as a dark revenant until she reclaims her body. Her husband now knows we have come."

"Her husband?" Kai said.

"Arxani, as she said. You must learn one thing, Kai. The lesser undead, like these…" She motioned to the iron-collared corpses. "They can perish. The lesser Ulfr, too, can fade away. But the powerful—the champions of death, the witches, the dark lords and the dark ladies—they will not die until the Great Witch is slain, and her spell is ended."

"A mighty woman, she must be," Kai uttered. The highlands surrounding him seemed so empty, now, but it was the silence before a great storm.

"She is the most powerful magic-weaver living," Gudrun said, "or un-living."

CHAPTER TWO

"Night falls over Badelgard."

Gudrun's ominous words only chilled Kai further as the sun set and its already meager heat dissipated.

Against all odds, they had reached what Gudrun had called "the forest of the damned." What once had been a wooden wall was now a blackened, burned ring of ash. The gray ruins of a tower lay on the edge. Quickly, Kai realized where they were. As a scout, he heard stories of the "Haunted Forest" that lay in the shadow of the mountains: a dark, an evil place where nightmares and the bad dreams of men came alive.

"Some called it the Darkling Wood," Gudrun explained. "For many years, the lord of White Wolf Keep appeased the evil, giving it human sacrifices in exchange for their never venturing past the wall. But appeasement only works for so long. In time the Great Witch returned in her un-living glory, and the darklings within answered her beckoning. So began the forever-winter."

"I have no respect for appeasers," Kai said. "To face your enemy on the battlefield like a man… to die at the end of his sword, fighting… that is better than surrender."

Gudrun nodded. "But here is where the evil began. And here, Kai, we must go. You must learn the nature of the darklings and of the Ulfr. And we must do so before morning light. By then, the Fell Lord and his army will arrive, and even you cannot defeat him."

"I would not be so sure."

"Hubris is natural for the Dragon's Son. But you must listen to me, Kai. You have the strength of Fire and Salt, but I have the wisdom of the goddess."

At her boast, his wings turned rigid once again. It struck him how little control he had over his newfound body. Perhaps, the Green Dragon himself—now far in the west—had some measure of power over him. "All right, Gudrun," he said despite it all. "I will follow you into the Darkling Wood… into the Haunted Forest, as the scouts called it."

"Perhaps that is a more apt name. The darklings have fled into the land, but the forest remains haunted."

He took his first steps over the burnt ring of ash and debris where the wall once had stood. The snow crunched underneath his well-worn boots. Gudrun followed just a step behind.

The last rays of the sun glanced off the black pine-boughs. The Darkling Wood lay silent, but Kai sensed in his heart that it was not empty.

The mountain peaks—forming a dark, looming shape in the absence of light—stretched far above the pines. The only sounds were the footsteps of Kai and Gudrun, crunching against the powdery snow. That, and whispers.

The whispers were so faint that Kai wondered if he imagined them. Yet they were there, in his mind—real or otherwise—a compilation of words that did not form complete thoughts, the ravings of the insane or perhaps the grievances of the unquiet dead.

"Your first lesson." Gudrun's voice startled him, breaking the long half-silence. "Places like the Darkling Wood, or Blackfold... epicenters of evil. They are, by their nature, locations where evil deeds were committed, or where the dead refuse to move on. Tell me, Kai, what you hear in this place."

"Whispers," Kai answered, and the whispers seemed to grow louder.

"Whispers, indeed. The whispers of those long dead. An evil deed was committed here... actually, many evil deeds. Hundreds, thousands, perhaps millions. Year after year. Long ago, these woods were considered sacred by the Ulfr witches. The witches, you see, served as priests. And the Great Witch who haunts us now—Enara—was the greatest of them all. She discovered a way to grant herself eternal life. By the time the dragon burned her away on the fields of Blackfold, she had lived for many hundreds of years."

There was only darkness in the spaces of the pines, but Kai sensed the listening ears of many thousands. He continued through the snow as a building, almost-tangible weight filled the air.

"In elder years far removed from history, there was a shrine in this forest. A stone altar lay in its center. It was devoted to the Great Mother, and her High Priestess presided over it. Each year, a lottery was held across the land. Woe to the mother who was chosen. To have her child wrested from her care and taken to the shrine, to the stone altar, and the High Priestess—wielding a ritual knife—"

"Enough!" Kai roared. "I know what you are going to say. I don't want to hear it. I know the Ulfr are wicked."

Gudrun continued. "Enara, the Great Witch, has the blood of many hundreds of thousands on her hands. Innocent lives, snuffed out. The great families—the witches, the dark lords and dark ladies—were exempt from the lottery. That is why you hear whispers. They are driven mad with grief, with horror. They are desperate. Their words do not make sense to you, Kai, but I know what they want. They want to be released from this prison. They want to help you defeat the Great Witch."

"And how can I help them?" Kai choked on his words as the full weight of the children's grief pressed over him. "How can I help them?" he repeated.

"Follow me," Gudrun said, and led him deeper into darkness.

As they walked, the shadows seemed to press in, growing somehow closer and more tangible.

"What are the Ulfr?" Kai said. "Where do they come from?"

"The first Ulfr," Gudrun began, "were exiles. Some Elvenking sent them away from their homeland. Sorelas was the patriarch's name. Anué was his sister-wife. Some writings about them were in the library at Oskir, though now all the books—and the Golden House itself—has burned down, as you know. Their early years are lost to history… but we can only guess that they were religious exiles. That the Elvenking disliked their worship of the Great Mother, and banished him for that purpose."

"You are from the realm of the gods," Kai said. "Surely you know."

"I will only tell you what you need to know," Gudrun said. "I will only tell you what is necessary to set things right."

"Where are you taking me? Surely you can tell me that." The whispers continued, louder than ever but just as meaningless.

"The spirits have remained in the wood for time beyond remembrance. Their anguish created the dark stain on the forest. But something else took this power and forged it into evil."

"Just tell me, by the gods!" Kai roared. His wings again stood erect. His breath felt hot. And at the same time, the building weight of the forest grew to a pinnacle. The heaviness of the little children—their terror, their despair, as they beheld the ritual-knife—reached its full volume, as the boughs of the pines gave way to a silent, snowy clearing in the woods.

CHAPTER THREE

A wrecked altar lay in the center of the clearing. Without Gudrun's warnings, it would appear a pile of stones. Gudrun began walking toward it, but Kai stopped at the eaves of the pines.

Gudrun turned, girt fully in her battle-maiden gear and holding her spear proudly. "Come here. It is not fitting for a dragon to cower in the shadows."

Her words stung him. His breath again flared. He still wished to hide in the pine eaves under a cloak of darkness, but his legs carried him forward of their own accord. Another power, another self, would not allow him to hide.

"Here it is," Gudrun said. "The center of the Darkling Wood, the source of its sorrow. Now surely, Kai, you want to know how you can free these souls from their prison."

Kai sighed. "If it will stop the whispering, then yes, I want to know."

"The Great Mother bound them here, and used their anguish to indwell the darklings. Therefore, you must speak to her." Gudrun held out her left hand, and with her spear, sliced open her wrists. The blood fell voluminously, gushing red onto the altar.

"Gudrun!" Kai screamed. "I can't do this without you!"

As the blood fell onto the stone, a steam-like vapor wafted up. Slowly it began to take shape.

Kai ran up to Gudrun as she sank into the snow. "I can't do this without you!" he screamed. "You are my last friend left! I am alone!" He realized, despite everything, that he loved her.

"Look!"

Gudrun collapsed.

A tall shape loomed above Kai. The steam from Gudrun's blood had formed an apparition. In height, she stretched to the tips of the pines. Her hair, though long, was bald in patches and sparse. The hollows of her eyes went deep, ending in beady black orbs. Her skin was wrinkled and pruned. Her teeth were twisted and needlelike. Her body was clothed in hide, before it trailed off into the steam-like mist.

Here she was: the Great Mother that the Ulfr worshipped, glutted with sacrifices. "Who has summoned me?" she proclaimed.

"Kai Riverhall," he said. He felt naked without a sword, though a steel weapon would do him no good. He wrung his hands.

"Not one of my followers." Her eyes were expressionless beads, impossible to read. "A human, rather. What do you want?"

"I want you to pay for your crimes."

The Great Mother's expression did not change, if she even felt emotions at all. "Strange," she said. "I had thought Enara demolished all resistance… that the humans were enslaved, or killed. I had thought…"

"Perhaps you should not think," Kai said. "I have the blood of the Green Dragon." He wasn't sure what Gudrun wanted him to say, how she wanted him to accomplish the goals set out before him. With as confident a voice as he could muster, he shouted, "You are beholden to me! I demand you relinquish these children. I demand you release your grip on their souls! Let them go!"

The Great Mother gasped. Kai wondered if her eyes were sightless, if they were as blind as they appeared. But nonetheless, she spoke. "A human, you are. You think yourself far above your station. The humans were born from slime long ago, and they remain slime in my eyes. Do you realize who you speak to, Kai Riverhall?"

"I said, release them!" He was acting on a guess, that Gudrun had summoned her for a reason. He would speak with as much confidence as he could muster. "The Green Dragon has given me his blessing! I am not slime! I demand you release these children, you vile-hearted hag! You will answer to me!"

She gasped again. Her brows furrowed. She bared her tangled, twisted teeth. "How dare you!" she hissed. "Know that you are a worm, Kai Riverhall, and I will not answer to you!"

"But you will answer to the Green Dragon, and his blood is in me! The Green Dragon did not fully destroy you. But he has returned in me! I command you once again, *release them!*"

She pitched back her ghostly, vaporous hand and struck at Kai.

Kai grabbed at her, and no one was as surprised as him when he restrained her successfully, and his mortal fingers were wrapped around her ethereal wrist. A voice spoke from within him, a voice he never knew he had. Bestial, hoarse, yet louder than his loudest scream, he looked into the Great Mother's eyes and answered in his new voice: "Long ago, when I left this land with the human on my back, you promised you would never haunt it again. You promised you would lie dormant. You promised you would fall into eternal sleep. But did you?"

The Great Mother struck with her other clawed hand, but Kai caught it too. She shrieked like a winter gale. Her beady black eyes seemed to grow larger. Her twisted yellow teeth bared in a snarl.

"Release them," the dragon spoke through Kai, "or I will destroy you according to our oath. Do not test me, Skolla!"

Skolla—perhaps that was her name. It did not matter. The Great Mother—goddess or no—was screaming now, and the shrillness of her voice caused the shadows of the dead children to retreat. "Have some proper respect, you dog!" Her scream finally formed words. "Remember what you are: a human! You claim to be the blood of the Green Dragon, and you claim to speak for him! But it is all a *lie*. You are a human dog, the lowest of the low, and you must learn some proper respect!"

As if in answer to her accusation, a painful flaring-up began in Kai's knuckles and the tips of his fingers. He cried out but soon he realized the Green Dragon, or perhaps his spirit, was melding his flesh. Another stage of the transformation, another step closer to achieving dragon hood. His fingers, in painful spasms, turned to claws. They were razor sharp, the color of steel, and Kai knew they were certainly stronger and sharper than any metal.

With his new weapons, his grip seemed to tighten. The claws dug into the Great Mother's ghostly hands, and she shrieked in pain. Her teeth once again formed a snarl.

"Release them!" Kai thundered. His voice was not his own.

"Never!" she hissed. "I will never submit to a human dog!" She ripped free her hands, and the claws tore through her wrists. Her hands burst into ghostly vapor and disappeared. Handless, she backed away, but she was bound to the altar and could not go far. Kai followed her.

"Release them!" Kai repeated. "I will not wait much longer. You have taken the souls of these innocent Ulfr children. You have used their anguish to spread evil through the forest. You are the darkest villainess I have ever met, and the most frighteningly ugly crone I have ever seen."

"Among my sisters, your words would be a compliment," the Great Mother hissed. "My servant Thanara is not long-off. She, and her husband, will certainly spell your end."

"If she is not far off, and you will not obey me, then I must do my deed now! Prepare to die, Skolla, Great Mother. I will lift your curse from the Darkling Wood!"

"And yet you will not end my power," she hissed as Kai ran at her. "My throne is nearly pulled from the ice, and when that is done, I will be invincible."

At last he was upon her. With his newfound claws he dug into her chest and raked her. The Great Mother let out a shrill, wintry scream. The trees shook, and a low rumbling rose to a deafening roar. A circular wind blew a cyclone of snow around the altar. Screams echoed from deep within the wood. There was a loud sonic boom, and then all was silent. The cyclone of snow erupted into powder.

For the first time, the forest felt empty. The spirits of the children had vanished. Silence had fallen over the dark pine wood, but more than that, there was peace.

Kai realized he was not alone, though. The body of Gudrun still heaved with breath. Her blood—black from lack of life, for she had inhabited the body of a dead woman—stained the snow around her.

"My blessed Gudrun," he said. "I had once loved you. I still do."

"Take my armor," Gudrun said. "Take my helmet and my breastplate and my spear. Fly to Blackhelm Keep. I will meet you there, at our staging ground." She spat blood and fell still.

Immediately he obeyed her. He stowed her helmet in his pack, removed her breastplate after a lengthy struggle, and removed her spear from her limp grasp. He gazed at her blonde-streaked hair, and realized he had loved her.

A creeping feeling made him realize the peace had left. A new presence had entered the wood. He looked up and saw what could only be a Fell Lord. Thanara's husband, girt in mournful black plate.

If a man, he was the tallest of all the living. Yet his burning red eyes, smoldering from within the greathelm of black steel, betrayed his identity as something entirely different. In both of his black steel gauntlets, he gripped a giant white sword edged with frost. When he spoke, Kai heard the Badelgardic tongue, but guessed that the Fell Lord spoke in a tongue that all could hear. "Look at what you have done," Arxani said. "You have committed a black deed. You have disrupted the power of the forest. And now you must pay."

Kai knew that Gudrun would want him to flee. To fly away, across the peaks and across the Ice Shelf to the stronghold of Blackhelm Keep. But looking into those burning red eyes, a fire had begun to burn within him. When Kai—blood of the Green Dragon—was challenged, he could not help but answer it. "It is you that should surrender. I have the Green Dragon inside me. He has entered my body so that I can make your people's destruction complete."

The smoldering red eyes flared brighter for an instant. The glow of his white sword increased and a chill emanated from its frosted edges. "A thousand dooms upon you. Dragon or no, I will destroy you, and you will never know the peace of death. You will be raised as a lord of bones, or a hungering corpse, or a morguis, under the command of Lady Thanara."

At the mention of her name, a hiss echoed through the trees and Kai saw the dark lady's revenant leering at them from the distance. If she ever had any beauty, it was gone; in un-life, her face matched her heart. An ancient crone of the night, she was: eye-sockets sunk deep, sparse gray hair, a snarling visage.

Kai flapped his wings and flew at the Fell Lord in a burst of speed. But despite his newfound strength, Arxani did not move in the slightest. He stood erect like an iron tower, and smote Kai with his steel gauntlet.

Kai went flying backward and hit the ground with an audible thump. Arxani charged, pitching back his frosty blade and preparing to strike. The edges of the sword glowed as he charged with thunderous steps. Kai stood up, prepared to lay his claws into the black steel, but was struck.

The blade slashed an inch deep into Kai's unprotected ribs, and filled him with such a chill that it nearly extinguished the dragon-fire within him. But as soon as the blow landed, green scales ripped over his skin like pox, and ensured the Fell Lord's wound was shallow.

Kai cried out in pain. Despite the unearthly chill, his anger burned brighter than ever. With both hands he tore downward, scratching along the Fell Lord's black armor and leaving white claw-marks. At last, he fell into the snow, but he did his best to take the Fell Lord with him, laying hold of his sabaton and yanking as hard as he could.

At last, some luck: the Fell Lord tripped over Kai's hands, toppling over like the steel tower he was. The impact sent a wave of cold through the forest. Arxani screamed, and his white sword fell from his grasp and clattered through the snow.

Kai worked his claws relentlessly, trying to pierce the black steel armor, but it would not come undone. He was certain his claws would shred regular steel armor, but this was of a strange make. Perhaps, judging by the tortured faces forged on the metal, it was made through some dark ritual or ancient alchemical secret. Its origin did not matter. The only thing that mattered was piercing it; the only thing that mattered was slaying Arxani.

Kai reached for the white blade. Arxani followed, but was too late. Kai's hand—now green and covered in scales—touched the hilt. Immediately a freezing white flame burst around it, scalding his hand with cold. He drew back, and considered taking to the skies and flying to Blackhelm Keep. But he could not. He would not. Until the Fell Lord was dead, the fire within him would never calm itself.

He raked his claws against the steel armor with more force than ever. He put every ounce of his energy into the shredding of the black steel—crying out with each heave of his dragon-claws—and just as he began to make progress, the Fell Lord stood up like a tower out of the sea. Kai went tumbling into the snow as Arxani laid hold once again of the fell white blade.

Kai flew at him with all his strength. He aimed a little too high, striking Arxani's upper chest. Not sure of what to think, he heaved his hand round the Fell Lord's black-steel helmet and flapped his wings again, continued the jaunt.

To his surprise, the helmet broke free. Kai tumbled through the snow with it wrapped in his hand. He stumbled to his feet, throat burning from exertion, panting like mad. The Fell Lord Arxani stood there helmetless.

To call the topmost portion of his body a head seemed a stretch to Kai: a dusty, round black stump it seemed, crawling with bugs of all kinds—a maggot there, a centipede there, and a worm wriggling from what could only assume to be an eye. Even a dark-hearted crone like Thanara seemed too good to wed an ancient corpse like this.

But regardless—after a second's stunned silence—Kai realized he had to finish the deed. He threw the black greathelm on the ground, and a psychic shudder echoed through the trees. He got a running start and then leapt toward the unmasked Fell Lord with the assistance of his wings. With the back of his scaled hand, Kai struck Arxani.

The head burst into dry tomb-ash and the bugs that indwelled it went flying. As Kai landed with both feet and turned around, the Fell Lord's plates of armor fell to pieces. As his body crumbled to dust, his wife—the revenant—let out a moan. His white blade, once glowing with frost, faded into a dull, colorless gray.

Breaking branches and hushed murmurs indicated an Ulfr war-band was coming. They would arrive to find their leader dead. Kai wondered if, deep down, they would be pleased.

He grabbed blessed Gudrun's armor and her spear. He flapped his wings and leapt into the sky, and his feet did not touch the ground.

CHAPTER FOUR

The peaks of the mountains lay before him. With the assistance of Gudrun he had purged the Darkling Wood of its evil. But he knew the most difficult task lay ahead.

He flew beside the snowy peaks, beside the purple-ridged rock of the Dragonteeth range. To the north, past these towering beauties, lay the land of the elves which—despite its proximity—hardly any Badelgard folk had visited.

It struck him that he was flying through the sky, and that never in a thousand lifetimes would he have thought it possible. But below him, to the south, he caught occasional glimpses of the Ice Shelf, the center-point of the Ulfr's evil will. Whenever the gray ice appeared through the obscuring mountain peaks, a sound half-sonic and half-mental shuddered through Kai's mind, like the wail of the entombed Great Mother. Kai had a feeling he did not defeat her, only that he freed the souls of those children and banished her spirit from the Darkling Wood. He had a sense he would see her again.

The winds blew in freezing gusts this high up. Several times, howls pierced the air; this was the realm of the White Wolves, and the packs ran free here. Few could face a White Wolf in combat, and Kai doubted even the strongest warrior in Varda could face a whole pack.

When morning broke, and the sun arose in its bronze glory, a green sea of pines appeared below. Far in the distance was Frost Lake—a blue shape against the snow—and somewhere by its shores was Blackhelm Keep.

Soon it appeared in view. The Blackhelms—according to some, the strongest warriors of all the noble houses—had built a citadel worthy of their reputation. Kai had never strayed this far from home, from the realm of the scouts, nor had he spoken with anyone who had. But when two rings of high stone walls appeared, and—in its center—a large cluster of straw-thatched homes, he knew he had reached his destination.

As he descended, careful to land with more grace than the past, the dark shapes below him formed people. Outside the walls, a black mass took the shape of an army. He realized that Blackhelm Keep was under siege.

In time, he landed. There were few people within the central town. All looked pale, thin, emaciated. The bone-thin finger of hunger seemed to have touched Blackhelm Keep. It was natural, of course; thanks to the wintry summer, the crops had all failed. And if Kai had not been given this new body, this new self, then the hunger would have begun to affect him long ago.

In the main thoroughfare, the few starved people—an elderly man at death's door and his wife, and a few children shaking from hunger or cold—gawked at him. It took a few moments before Kai remembered he had changed. He was not himself any longer. A pair of green wings now sprung from his back, and his hands had turned to claws. Perhaps if he looked at his reflection in Frost Lake, he would see yellow reptilian eyes.

But it did not matter. Despite his aberrant appearance, the people here were too starved and desperate to sound any kind of alarm. In time they looked away, probably discounting Kai's appearance as another phantasm of this fell winter, a herald of the end of days.

Kai walked through the narrow streets of Blackhelm Keep. Gudrun had told him to come here, that she would meet him. She had called this place a "staging ground."

A stone castle rose above the thatched roofs of the houses. Here, Sigmund Blackhelm had once ruled over the region of Trowheim. That was before he took the throne, before he moved to the much more beautiful and luxurious—or so it seemed—Golden House. Then, at some point in the confusion of this eternal winter, he had passed on. The succession of rulers had led to Queen Kenna, and then the palace itself had finally burned down. Who knew what happened now? Who held the throne of Badelgard, if even there was a king or queen alive?

As Kai walked the snow-buried streets, a noise echoed through the area: a rusting hinge, a grating sound. In the distance, through a small thoroughfare, the gate to the inner wall had cracked open slightly. A lithe figure slinked through: a woman, short, with long black hair and a sword in her hand that dripped with blood. She ran down the street; her gray eyes met Kai's, and he knew in that instant that it was Gudrun. Even if he looked past the mortal wound in her chest, he would have seen the light of Altgard in her eyes. Gudrun had assumed another body.

"Kai," she said, putting all his doubts to rest. "Blackhelm Keep is the last stronghold. The men have fought bravely. But the siege will not last much longer." Her voice was different—lighter, more feminine perhaps—but it had the same steely resolve of a valkyrie that Kai recognized. "Some distant relative of Sigmund is in charge, now. He is braver than his predecessor, though. He is commanding the defense personally."

"I have your gear, Gudrun."

She smiled. "Thank you, Dragon's Son. You have lifted the curse of the Darkling Wood, I assume."

Kai nodded.

Her smile grew. "It has all gone as I hoped. I will do my best to help you, Kai, but remember I am only a guide. Long ago, the gods made a treaty: that they would not interfere directly in the affairs of mortal men. I must follow it, though I would love to follow you in battle, and fight alongside you."

Kai smiled. "Whether you are a guide or a warrior, the fact remains: I could not have done it without you." Despite the shift in her appearance, the same light of Altgard gleamed in her eyes. Her manner of speech had not changed. He still loved her. "I love you," he said.

Gudrun smiled. Her new cheeks flushed with color. "If only I could love you, Dragon's Son. But I cannot. Even in your new form, I see you heart of gold, your beauty of soul. But the time for love is over. A terrible task awaits us."

"What is that?"

"We must go to the Ice Shelf," Gudrun answered. "We must face the Great Witch. We must end her spell, or else the winter will continue, and Badelgard will never be as it was."

"I doubt it will ever be as it was, even if we succeed."

"You speak truth." Gudrun smiled. "But now I must don my gear. Then we will depart. To the Ice Shelf, and to eradicate the Ulfr from the earth."

From the castle of Blackhelm Keep—the staging ground, as Gudrun said—Kai waited for her command. He did not know how to picture the evil on the Ice Shelf. He had seen trolls; he had seen Ulfr, and Fell Lords unmasked. But the center-point of Ulfr evil, from which all the darkness of the fell winter emanated… that he had never seen, and he could only imagine how it would appear to mortal eyes.

When the new Gudrun appeared out of the darkness of an alley, she looked somehow more like a valkyrie than she had before. Despite her small size, her dark hair and lithe physique, the bravery of a battle-maiden and the courage of Altgard lighted from her silver eyes. Her legs, though thin, seemed as immovable as the roots of the mountains. A whiff of mountain meadows and high gales seemed to swirl around her. She seemed, for once, to have achieved her purpose. She was the embodied valkyrie, a proud daughter of Vana.

"What is your command, Gudrun?" Kai asked.

"The Ice Shelf awaits," she answered.

Gudrun the Battle-Maiden mounted Kai's back, wrapping her knees firm around his scaly sides. Then, once more, Kai leapt into the air, and once more, his feet did not touch the ground.

It was not long before he was high enough to see the Ice Shelf. The gray mass stretched before him. A cloud hovered above it. A spear of blue lightning lit from deep within. Even from this far away, a sound could be heard: a dull groan that filled the mind, and the crackling of stone grating against ice.

CHAPTER FIVE

As soon as Kai passed under the dark cloud, and the gray ice of the shelf was below him, all light seemed to fade away. The light of day vanished, replaced in an instant with night. Soundless flashes of blue lightning provided brief illumination, but thunder did not answer them.

Flurries of gray snow filled the air. "Land," Gudrun ordered.

Silently, Kai obeyed, drifting downward as slowly as he could manage. At last, his feet touched the ice. He slipped for a second but quickly caught his footing. Gudrun hopped off. The dark cloud hung above him still. Another spear of blue lightning, soundless as always, flashed in the distance. A gale burst from the northwest.

He had arrived. There were no trolls, no Ulfr in sight. But—like the Darkling Wood before he righted the wrongs—he sensed that the Ice Shelf was far from empty.

Kai followed Gudrun through the flurries of gray snow. Without her guidance, Kai was certain he would get lost. But he followed her through the perpetual night. The journey lasted several hours and the power of the Ice Shelf soon numbed his body and his mind. The mental scream from its center pulsed through him continuously, and grew louder with each step. But he soldiered on like a true man of Badelgard, following the battle maiden on her dangerous trek.

Then, unexpectedly, when Kai had lost all sense of time, the journey ended. Another soundless blue flash illuminated the center of the Ice Shelf.

The statue of the Great Mother, in size, was like a mountain. The stone, carved into the shape of the enthroned goddess, was so large it seemed that someone had lifted a peak from its roots, planted it on the Ice Shelf and had a giant carve it into the proper shape.

The bottom left corner of the throne was still half-buried in the ice. In front of the statue, a countless horde of trolls—tied via cord to the monolith—roared as they tried to pull it out of its burial-place. It dawned on Kai that the psychic scream was pulsing from the statue, and that when the statue was fully free of the ice, its emanations would send even a dragon into madness.

"Here it lies," Gudrun whispered. "This is where the Great Mother had her throne, of old. How it got here, how something so large could be carved from stone… that is a secret unknown to mortal men."

The statue, from what Kai could see, had a strong resemblance to the ghost he fought. But now her likeness was as large as a mountain, and even in his new body, his new self, he couldn't help but feel powerless against her now.

Another silent spear of lightning pierced the darkness. The gray flurries thickened.

"We don't have much time," Gudrun said. "We must act now. We must face the Great Witch."

"Where is she?" Kai said. "I don't see her."

"She is probably in the air, flying around the statue and watching her plans unfold. She is powerful… more powerful than you. We must act wisely. We must meet her on her own terms, and speak with her."

Kai's flight seemed—in his mind—to take longer than his journey across the mountains. He had underestimated just how tall the statue was, even though it was not fully out of the ice.

Guided only by the brief blue flashes of lightning, Kai flew through the thick gray flurries. The closer he drew to the dark cloud, the poorer his eyesight seemed to become.

When at last he reached the top of the stone throne, he could see nothing. The gray flurries turned to moisture on his skin. He was flying in total darkness, and a knot formed in his stomach. It became harder to breathe. He was so cold. He started shivering. He realized he was afraid.

A light appeared. At first it was a faint spark, green in color, but soon it grew to a ball of flame and then to a bright, dazzling orb of light.

In its illumination, Kai Riverhall caught his first glimpse of the Great Witch, Enara.

Her hair hung to her hips in golden braids. Her eyes were blue, unlike the rest of her people. Her lips were white, as if from lack of blood. A long black robe dangled far below her feet. A white skull was embroidered on it.

"Enara," Kai said. His voice was steady despite his fear.

"Kai Riverhall, dragon." Her voice was emotionless as his, but louder and standing out clearly against the roars of the trolls below. "You have come to destroy my work." Her eyes appeared frozen, emotionless like glass, as if there were no person behind them. "If you try, you will die. Know that with a word, I could slay you. I have become a master of life and death. Before you blink your eyes again, I could kill you and raise you back as a revenant. But you have another choice."

"And what is that?" Kai's wings had begun to strain.

The witch did something Kai thought impossible: she smiled. "You could reign with me. You could sit with me on my throne. You could be the King of the Dead, and I could be your queen."

Kai gulped. His shivering grew more virulent. Perhaps, her ominous words had chilled the air. "You, the Queen of the Dead... and I, your husband? That is the offer you would make, correct?"

The witch seemed to hesitate. Then the word came from her lips like an extended sigh, like a prolonged cold wind: "Yes."

Gooseflesh spread over Kai's skin, but he knew what he had to say. "Lady Enara... the Great Witch, as they call you."

She smiled again.

"I have come to end your curse over Badelgard. I refuse your offer. I have come to destroy you, not to reign with you as king of the damned."

In a second's span, her strangely frozen faced turned to an expression of ultimate rage. She thrust her hand forward, and the pale green flame flared to an explosive size, lighting up the dark cloud. The strange flame would have melted Kai, but all around him the voices of children began to chant. The souls of the Ulfr children—perhaps hovering around them, now—extinguished the flame before it could burn Kai.

She screamed. "What is this? Who are you, Kai Riverhall? You say you are the Green Dragon... perhaps you speak truth! But who are these folk?"

"They are your own kind, Enara. They have turned against you. They were sacrificed to the Great Mother. Your end is near." His words seemed strangely empty to him. Indeed, even if they stopped the witch's green flame, even if they blocked all her spells, even if they removed her powers of flight and sent her plummeting to the ground... even then, it seemed the Great Witch would find some way to prevail, that she would cement the fell winter and her dark grasp would never leave the Ice Shelf, nor Badelgard.

Kai looked into her blue eyes, frozen and dead like those of a child lost in the mountains. He couldn't see any soul, any personhood, behind them, until he peered deeply into them. And there, in the black spaces of her eyes, he saw a woman of Ulfr lineage, gifted with such magic talent that she could be truly called a genius. Yet beyond this great talent that sat deep inside her, he saw an emptiness, a sadness so deep that fueled an ambition beyond any of her people. An ambition that drove her to seek after arcane secrets, to find ways to become the greatest wizard in the world. And when she achieved it, it wasn't enough. He saw a person driven to such lengths that she sought to cheat death. And she achieved her goal. And he saw a woman whose spirit remained long after her people were destroyed, long after the dragon had burned her civilization with fire. And then, deep within her frozen eyes, he saw a woman with a heart so cold, a spirit so remorseless, a soul so dead, that his wings ceased their movement and he fell back with a gasp, plummeting into the air in a breathless free-fall.

At last he righted himself, ascending once more with each flap of his wings. But he had looked into the eyes of the witch, and what he saw, he could never recover from. The children around him kept their chanting, but he would never forget the person he saw behind those frozen eyes. His shivering became even more pronounced.

The witch spoke. "Kai Riverhall. I already heard word from my spies across the realm. They call you Dragon's Son. They say you have the wings and eyes of a dragon. They were right. And I already felt your handiwork in the sacred forest. You overcame—by virtue of the dragon's spirit—the fragment of the goddess's soul that remained there. But know, Kai Riverhall, that you have no reason to be proud. The fragment of the goddess was just that—a mere fragment, an infinitesimal shard—and you will never overcome her. I have served her with my life. I have become her most zealous devotee." Despite her fiery speech, her expression seemed dead and frozen on the outside, if one did not peer deep into her eyes; and gods knew Kai would never do that again. "Know, Kai Riverhall, that the goddess cannot be overcome, not even if the Green Dragon himself were to fly back over the sea. Know, Kai Riverhall, that a choice stands before you. You may join me, Kai Riverhall, as my husband and my partner. You may sit upon the throne and share in my power. Either that, or your life will be snuffed out and then—in an instant!—re-instilled within you as a shadow of what it was. And you will wander Badelgard, or what remains of it, as one of the tortured, anguished dead."

Gooseflesh spread anew all over him. He whimpered. Yet a voice was speaking inside him, and the voice could not be stilled: *Do not heed the witch's speech-craft! Answer her guile and tricks of the tongue with violence and fire.*

Perhaps, Gudrun was telling him this. Perhaps, it was the dragon. But it did not matter. Regardless of who gave the advice, he would take it. The witch was trying to deceive him with her ingeniously-crafted words, her spoken threats. But a guileful tongue could not—as the voice said—argue with violence and fire.

Despite Kai's fear of the witch, his fear of the woman behind those eyes, he steeled himself and prepared to swoop at her and strike with his claws.

There was a commotion down below. The grating of ice against stone reached its pinnacle, and the trolls stopped their heaving. Their quieted voices led to silence, but it was only brief. The Seat of the Great Mother was fully pulled from its icy tomb. And after a moment's pause, the half-sonic, half-psychic scream emanating from the monolith reached a deafening zenith. The wail sent shudders through every inch of Kai's body and mind. Even Gudrun screamed.

To any mortal—and to Kai, before his transformation—the sonic emanations would be maddening. Despite the wordlessness of the pulsating barrage, the command of the goddess's scream seemed clear: *Throw yourself off a precipice, human vermin! But before you do, kill everyone you love!*

The thought of it sickened him. Even as the dragon's own son, the psychic shudder caused him—for a brief second—to lapse into free fall. But his wings, perhaps not of his own design, began flapping again, taking him higher and higher until he was eye-level with the Great Witch.

"It is complete," Enara said. Her fingers had grown long and green, like vines; perhaps she, like Kai, was undergoing a transformation. Perhaps she was becoming something like her goddess: an ancient, evil-hearted crone. "It is done! My goal is realized!" She sounded ecstatic. "The time of the Ulfr has been renewed! It is done! It is done!" At the same time as her joy, her frozen eyes fixed on Kai. "And you—you dog, you wolf!—if you think you will escape with your life, you must think again. You have refused an offer that many would impale themselves to achieve! You have refused your chance to rule with me as my husband, as the King of the Dead! Ha! Ha! You must be mad! No, you are not mad, for the goddess herself is mad. You are stupid, stupid like a dog! Yes! Yes! You are stupid!"

The sonic shriek from the stone seat was beginning to overcome

Kai. Perhaps, not even the strength of the Green Dragon could sustain him. The goddess that Enara worshiped was ancient and horrific to behold; intelligent beyond compare, and evil to the most infinitesimal part. But the Great Mother's strength was not in her intelligence or wit, nor was it in any supernatural power. The Great Mother's most fearsome quality, her biggest danger to mankind, was her madness: the senseless, raving, cackling madness that her stone Seat so overpoweringly embodied.

Kai was losing control. He was losing hope. The Green Dragon's power, his fiery rage, was dying away like a coal left un-tended. The Great Mother and her servant would prevail. He would wander Badelgard in a bleak existence, as—like Enara stated—one of the tortured dead.

He lifted his claws, flexed his hands, but even that seemed too great a struggle. Moving at all, even thinking, was a near impossible task in the path of the constant sonic shriek. It was a wonder he did not plummet to the ground; but the wings of the Green Dragon, perhaps moving of their own accord, continued to carry him aloft.

Blue lightning flashed around him—silent, as he expected—and in the brief light he saw the Great Witch's dead, frozen eyes were fixed on him with a zeal that made him gasp. "Kai Riverhall." Her voice boomed like thunder. "I will cast upon you a worse fate than any of the other humans. From now until the end of days, you will be my slave. I bind your life to mine. If I die, you die. If you take my life, you will lose yours. You will never escape my whips, my thumbscrews, the tortures I will devise." She cackled like her mad goddess. "I proclaim it: *Our lives are bound together, and forevermore!*"

Another shudder tore through Kai's body. This time it was more than a physical blow, or raw emotion. Every part of him—body, mind, and soul—was connected to this witch, whose eyes were so black and remorseless it was a wonder a person inhabited them.

Kai screamed as the witch's pronouncement was made real.

"We are bound together!" the Great Witch screamed. "You will never escape me! It is done! It is done! I have completed your mission,

O mother of our people! May the sacrifices begin again, and let the blood of the humans run for miles, up to the horses' bridles!"

As the witch shouted these words, Kai realized in his mind what he had to do, but also in his heart. He was bound—body, soul, and mind—to Enara. Their fates were intricately wrapped together, or so she had said. His index claw was sharper than steel. He let out a cry for all the men and women of Badelgard who had died. He let out another cry for the Ulfr children, sacrificed in the name of the cackling hag.

Then he slashed his wrist with his claw, and then slashed the other. The blood poured from his wounds and the life left him. His wings fell limp. He began to fall.

But Gudrun was carrying him. In his fading vision, he saw that the battle-maiden had sprouted wings. She was now like the valkyries in the children's stories. She was carrying him aloft, and letting him see the catastrophe—the triumph—unfolding.

"Enara!" Gudrun cried. "In your cold, calculating mind—in the black, bottomless chasm that is your soul—you never thought a man would sacrifice himself for the good of others! Your failure to understand the good present in the world has led to your downfall. Kai has sacrificed himself, and I can see that even now your life is fading. Your false life is leaving you! Yes, yes, you were right! It is done! It is finished, but not as you intended! And the Ulfr will pass on forevermore; your taint, long-dormant, will finally eradicate itself from Badelgard."

Kai could see the witch weakening. She did not go out with a scream, or a destructive spell. Instead, as all thought left her frozen eyes, she groaned—and Kai thought that, for a brief second, she realized what she had done. Her life was built around the destruction, the manipulation of others; and now, if anything awaited her at all it was the fires of damnation, or a worm-eaten grave that none would ever visit—not even her own people, or those she mistakenly called her friends.

As the witch's life left her, so too did her magic. She fell from the sky like an object. The trolls below began to melt. A group of Green Dragon priests revealed themselves, charging at the dying trolls with clubs.

And most importantly, perhaps, Kai felt the sonic emanations of the Great Mother's seat abruptly cease. A rumbling began, and the stone began to shake. It began to fall apart, bit by bit; first the nose, then the head, then the arms. The Seat of the Great Mother crumbled—no longer merely buried under the ice and hidden from view, but completely and utterly destroyed.

The priests were cheering below. The dark clouds overhead faded to nothing. Emptiness and silence ensued. The air grew warm. It began to rain.

Rain.

Kai died smiling.

PART FOUR:
WE ARE ALL KINGS

CHAPTER FIVE

Alysse had expected to bravely charge into the innumerable host, to maybe strike with her sword—and fumble—before a spear tore through her chest and she ended her life fighting evil. But it did not happen. A loud noise and a great wind blew from the north, from the Ice Shelf. The noise sent a shudder through Alysse's heart. But immediately the Ulfr around her stopped their fighting and looked in the direction of the sound.

She yanked the reins of the horse and halted the gallop. She wasn't sure what to think. It was well and good to perish in a last stand, to die fighting for a just cause. But first, she had to see what was going on. Vanquishing the enemy was her goal; becoming the heroine of "The Last Charge of Alysse Riverhall" and being sung-of all over Varda was not her highest priority.

The Ulfr were silent for much longer than she expected. For all intents and purposes, it seemed they had frozen—in fear, perhaps, or something else. They were all looking toward the Ice Shelf. Something was happening there, Alysse guessed. But she did not know, for the life of her, what it was.

Another wave of noise pulsed over them, but this one was a shudder of power, a shock-wave. And with it, all things related to the Ulfr seemed to fall apart.

The Ulfr men cried out and fell dead. In the span of seconds, their cheating of death reversed, and they rotted and aged into dry skeletons. The fearsome black armor of the Fell Lords fell into individual plates. The few Ulfr witches in the crowd met the same fate as the Ulfr men, turning into ancient skeletons.

And here Alysse stood, in the center of a pile of bones and the corpses of Sir Lirac and his warriors. It was as if she stood at the site of some great battle of man and Ulfr. They had cheated death, but at last justice was served. Something had happened on the Ice Shelf. Some brave hero had slain the Great Witch, or the Great Mother herself.

Something had happened there, and she did not know. But it didn't matter. For some reason, the humans had won. They had overcome the Ulfr. They had won!

The human slaves, bound in ball and chain—and kept as lure for the Ulfr's nefarious ends—began to cry out in relief. Tears of joy welled in their eyes.

Most importantly, and most immediately, the icy chill of this forever winter lifted. The air warmed. Alysse had survived the fell winter, and whether she deserved it she did not know. But she had survived. She began to cry.

"We have overcome!" she shouted. "I will come back to free you! The people are waiting for me! I will come back to free you!" She galloped off toward where the refugees were waiting. The snow glinted as it thawed. "We have overcome!" she cried out again. "We have overcome the Ulfr!"

By the time she reached the refugees, she was weeping. Tears had fallen all the way down her body and soaked her tattered green dress. But she was smiling, and the refugees were smiling too.

Women were embracing their husbands. Children were laughing. A few grown men wept like Alysse.

She shouted again, "We have overcome!" and her voice echoed down the river valley.

She was starving, and Alysse had no doubts the people were starving, too. There was no food. The crops had failed. Perhaps—after they freed the humans bound in chains—they would go to Andarr's Port, and take what ships they could. Perhaps Badelgard was a lost cause, but they had lived through the darkest time of their nation's history. Perhaps they—and Alysse with them—would live the rest of their lives as peasants in Zarubain. But they had overcome the Ulfr.

"We have overcome!" Alysse cried out again.

The refugees cheered.

Once the former slaves were freed of their bonds, Alysse led them and her people down the sides of the river valley. It grew steeper as she rode. Though they called her Queen of Badelgard, she did not feel superior to them in any way. They had suffered as she suffered. They had been through as much, if not more, than she had. If they cast her off, declared she was no longer their queen, then she would not fight it.

But as the river appeared below, snaking through the snow-covered aspens, she knew they had drawn near Andarr's Port, and the castle where she once had ruled.

She looked up at the sky. The sun was gone, and silver clouds hung above them. She expected more snow, and pelting ice, but once again the gods surprised her. Rain began to fall. *Rain.*

It felt strangely warm. Alysse could not remember the last time it had rained. Perhaps the snow would melt. She could only hope.

"It is raining! The fell winter is ended!" a man began to shout. "All hail Queen Alysse!"

The crowd followed: "All hail Queen Alysse! All hail Queen Alysse!"

Alysse's cheeks flushed hot. "Thank you... thank you, my people." But they were starving. Even now Alysse's hands trembled. The meager provisions they had eaten were not enough. Now, even a fisherman's stew from a Zarube peasant seemed a royal feast. Ah, she was so hungry.

Down the road she trotted, and the people followed. The aspens were gray against the melting snow. So many villages lay abandoned: there was Garn's Hole, its humble longhouses abandoned; there was Utja Thorpe, its fisheries and docks bereft of people. The winter had been fell indeed, but it was over. It had ended as suddenly as it began.

Finally Andarr's Port appeared. The brightly-colored longhouses appeared just how they were when Alysse left them. The darklings did not burn the city, perhaps thanks to their fear of fire. Alysse remembered how so many of them had perished when Harald set the Church of Umbra alight. Her god was certainly displeased, though perhaps—in high heaven—the lord of shadows understood.

As she passed through the open gate, the bodies of the darklings had turned to skeletons, perhaps in the same way as the Ulfr men from before. Alysse bit her lip lightly; the darklings had not turned back to their former selves. They had gone on to the afterlife, to Heaven or Hell, and there was no hope of ever seeing Harald again. The fell winter had claimed so many of the Badelgarders and only a remnant clung on to life. But it was time to move on, to go to another land and live the rest of their lives in servitude. But they would always share the memories, the stories of the brave deeds during Badelgard's darkest hour, and perhaps that was enough consolation.

Then she looked into the bay, and couldn't believe what her eyes beheld.

A fleet waited there in the silver waters. On the tall ships' sails, the Red Hawk of the Voraignes flapped in the gentle wind. Her father, Ergould, had likely come, and so too had her brother Lourges. They had come to make her pay for what she did—of that, she was certain—but Alysse would not let them punish the people of Badelgard. She had committed the crime, not them. If they wanted to take her away, to put her in some grim Zarubad prison, then she would go without a fight.

Through a veil of rain, a group of smaller ships appeared. The tall ships could not dock in the shallow waters of the bay.

At the front of this miniature fleet, in a wooden boat, her brother Lourges and her father Ergould approached. The green eyes of Lourges peered at Alysse, impossible to read.

In time they docked. Lourges stepped out, his face grim. Ergould followed quickly after.

Lourges walked up to Alysse. A familiar headband held up her brother's blond hair. A hauberk emblazoned with a hawk fell to his feet, and a thick Zarube-style longsword hung from his belt in a sheath. "Sister," he said.

Alysse bowed her head. "I have committed a crime against my family, against my House."

"You have," Lourges said. "You have stolen from the treasury, depleted our army, all for the sake of the northmen barbarians. You deserve to be locked up, tried for treason."

A tear fell from Alysse's eyes, but this time it wasn't from joy. She could not meet her brother's gaze; she was too ashamed.

"Look at me," Lourges said.

At last she did look up, gazing into her brother's beautiful green eyes. For once she saw warmth. He was smiling. "But we will do no such thing. I could no more harm my sister than cut off my own hand. I forgive you, and father forgives you."

Alysse fell into his embrace, and began to weep again—this time from joy. "Bless you, brother. Bless your heart."

"We have heard ill tidings from Badelgard. We have heard it is locked in a ceaseless winter, that its crops have failed and its people are starving. We have brought food, sister. As many sacks of flour as we could afford. As many salty hams as we could carry on the ship. It is all yours. We have also brought our swords, and as many soldiers as could safely leave the duchy. We have heard the nation of Badelgard is under attack."

"Bless you, brother," Alysse wept. "Bless you, father. The nation is no longer under attack. Our enemies have faded away as soon as they came. Like ghosts, they entered Badelgard and, like ghosts, they left."

"Then the strength of arms is not necessary. But all people need food, and we have brought as much to last you through the winter."

"Bless you, brother." Alysse couldn't stop weeping. "Will you accompany us to Oskir, the City of Kings, brother? I do not know what kind of fate has befallen our capital. The palace has burned to its foundations."

"I will accompany you to wherever you desire, sister," Lourges said. "I love you. Father and I will fight for you, and follow you wherever you need; to the gates of Hell and beyond."

Through her teary vision, she made out Ergould smiling just as warmly. The venerable Duke Vis Voraigne wore a fur hat and a long purple robe trimmed with sable. He had dressed for cold, but the fell winter ended just before he arrived. Perhaps the surprise was a pleasant one. How could it not be?

Oskir awaited them.

By the time they reached the uplands above the deep river-valley, the rain had washed away the snow. The brown grass now lay bare. The air was warm, so wonderfully warm, as they followed the road to Oskir. Behind Alysse and the former denizens of Oskir, a train of Zarubes traveled in the wake: horses heavy-laden with sacks of flour and salty meat; food that would get them through the coming winter, so that—in the warmth of spring—the people of Badelgard could pull themselves back on their feet and start a new chapter in their nation's history. Alysse was certain the fell winter had split the history of Badelgard in two. The second part was just beginning. The Ulfr were no more.

They pitched tents that night somewhere not far from Oskir, and Alysse fell asleep to the patter of rain.

In late morning the walls of Oskir appeared. King's Falls had thawed, and now gushed down in spite of the time of year. Up on King's Hill, the Golden House was a black, smoking ruin. But the Ulfr had vanished, and the homes of low-town had not caught fire. Perhaps the remains of the Golden House lay as a reminder: King Sven and King Sigmund had failed to defend their nation and people; Queen Kenna had never tried, and now there was a new ruler. Alysse was High Queen, now, and she had to succeed where the others had failed. She had to rebuild Badelgard, though it would prove a difficult task. The Great

Witch's spell had wrought such havoc on Alysse's people that they would have to rebuild from the foundations.

The sound of the gushing river, its ice partially thawed, reminded Alysse of just how much things had changed. The fell winter had ended. She pulled the reins of the horse and turned around as the people began to enter through the gate. Their clothing was tattered and muddy, and many looked sick. But the dark dream was over.

"People of Badelgard!" she shouted. Her brother, at the front of the line, smiled at her. "Eat as much as you want. Go to your homes, and rest. Tonight, at twilight, we will hold a meeting upon the ruins of the Golden House. It is a time for new beginnings, and everyone—lowborn and high—will have their say."

A few smiled, but most were too weary to react. Alysse motioned her father and brother to follow her, and then she began the steep ascent to Earls' Court.

Inside the Riverhall guesthouse, she began a fire. She rubbed her hands in the newfound warmth. The fire was so bright, so warm. All the chill that suffused her—the creeping cold that infiltrated her bit-by-bit through the evil winter—was thawed away, exorcised like a ghost. Ergould pulled a seat up to the fire, and Lourges followed in quick order. The fine chairs had not been looted. But the Ulfr did not seem to value gold or fine furnishings like humans did.

"My daughter," Ergould said, "you are a brave girl. I assume you have fought too hard to leave this place and come with us. I can only guess you do not wish to return to Voraigne Manor."

"Oh, I wish I could." Alysse reveled in the fire's warmth. "But I would never abandon my people at their most desperate hour. They have elected me High Queen, and I can't disappoint them. They need a leader to help them rebuild. I do not have a palace or a throne to sit on, but I am still their ruler."

"You are a good woman," Lourges said. "I am sorry, sister, if I said anything that hurt you."

"Even if you did, I understand." The flame was so bright, so warm. "I deserve your scorn. I am incredibly thankful that you did not take me away… throw me in a Zarubad prison, like I deserve."

"Daughter," Ergould said, "I must ask: What do you intend to say at this meeting?"

"It will be a surprise," Alysse said, though even she did not know.

She spent the whole day by the fire. At noon, she had her fill of salty ham. Below, in low-town, the scent of baking bread wafted up into the earls' guesthouses. She realized, as she spent time with her family, that without them they would have starved. If Lourges and Ergould had not forgiven her—if they had not brought these provisions—Alysse and her people would have either died slow deaths, or become the lowest of servants. Now, thanks to her brother and father, Badelgard had another chance, a new beginning.

The day slowly waned. It was late afternoon when Alysse walked outside for the first time. The air no longer had the bitter bite of winter. The rain had stopped, but the air remained warm.

In the distance, over the fields beyond Oskir's wall, a few dozen men—young and old—were running toward the gate. They wore crude leather leggings and, for the most part, no shirts. Alysse recognized a heavy brown-bearded man as the High Dragonpriest. And, with a gasp, she recognized two blond-haired boys with lovely blue eyes: her sons, Forni and Jarni; or, as they called themselves now, Razorclaw and Whitefang. The Green Dragonpriests had come.

Alysse would welcome them at the meeting.

CHAPTER SIX

It was shortly before twilight when the High Dragonpriest arrived in Earls' Court. Forni and Jarni were with him, but the other minor priests were not. They met her outside the Riverhall guesthouse, in the central courtyard.

"My lady, Alysse Riverhall, High Queen," the High Dragonpriest thundered. "I bring you good news on two fronts. One: the Great Witch is defeated, slain by the dragon's own son; the Seat of the Great Mother has collapsed, and the Darkling Wood is purged of its evil; and the Ice Shelf is melting."

"Melting?" Alysse said in disbelief.

"The other good news is this: I have done much searching of my soul, and in the end, I have determined to grant your request. Word has reached me you are High Queen of Badelgard, but without any heirs. I would do our nation no good if I kept Razorclaw and Whitefang for myself. I give them back to you: Forni and Jarni Riverhall, heirs to the High Throne."

"Thank you." Alysse smiled. Her sons' sullen blue eyes had seen much war and bloodshed. They would not have the social graces of the highborn; but perhaps that was a good thing. After all, they did not rule over the soft southlands, living in the lap of luxury. They were sons of Badelgard, tough and proud, earning a hard living for the soil. She had never known her sons, but she would try her best to know them now.

On the blackened ruin of the Golden House, every man and woman of Oskir was in attendance. Alysse did not know when the last time a meeting of lowborn and high convened; and surely it was the first time it happened on King's Hill.

She sat on the saddle of her horse, and the people surrounded her. Forni and Jarni gazed at her from the front. In the distance, Lourges and her father watched her, smiling.

"People of Badelgard," Alysse said, "our nation lies in ruins. We stand on the smoking remnant of the king's palace. People all over our realm have been cut down, and we are among the few that remain. Trowfell Keep is likely empty, and the Ulfr flung Carolyn Trowfell to her death. The other keeps, and the other earls, are probably not much better off. Our crops have failed. Food has run dangerously short. I led a foreign army into Badelgard, hoping to save it, but its leader turned against me.

"Our people lived their lives for hundreds of years ignoring the evil that lurked around them. We pretended the malice of Blackfold did not exist. The cowardly earls—unbeknownst to the common lowborns—fed the evil in the Darkling Wood; they appeased it and did not fight it. We, the people of Badelgard, have borne the punishment of these cowardly lords and ladies. It is not fair. It is not right. But at last, we have good news. Someone—somewhere—took a stand. Somehow, the Great Witch was defeated. And now the evil that lurked under the ice, or within the shadows of the pines, or under the hillocks of Blackfold… it is not hidden or tucked away, or appeased. It is defeated. The Ulfr are gone, and they will never return. Their taint is eradicated from the land. Not hidden, not covered-up, but destroyed. Our nation is in shambles, but the Enemy is gone."

A few in the crowd cheered. For the first time, Alysse saw a half-smile on her sons' faces.

"It is up to us to rebuild!" Alysse shouted. "I will not presume to call myself your queen. I will lead if you wish it, but only if you wish it."

"All hail Queen Alysse!" a man called out.

"But if I am queen," she continued, "if I sit on the High Throne of Badelgard, I want to be clear. The history of Badelgard is divided in two. Now, after the fell winter, I want to make a proclamation: from now on, there is no lowborn or highborn. Or, perhaps more accurately: there is only highborn. Everyone here—every pauper and peasant farmer—I proclaim you highborn. We are all kings! We are all queens! It is a new beginning. And if you say I am the High Queen, then know that even if you do not sit on the throne of Badelgard, you are highly born. You have survived the darkest hour of our nation's history. We are all highborn. We are all kings!"

"All hail Queen Alysse!" a woman shouted.

The crowd repeated the chant. "All hail Queen Alysse!"

"The winter is coming, but it will not be like it was!" Alysse continued. "I urge you, fellow highborns, that when the spring comes, we must set to work. Everyone that is able must do his best. We must build everything back to full strength. Each man is the king of his own land. Every man has the title of 'King,' and every woman, 'Queen.' And when we are at our full strength, and our granaries overflow, then we must forge swords and axes, and shirts of chain. We must ensure that no one can threaten us again! At our heart, we are a warrior people. And we, as a warrior people, must be ready for battle. Everyone here has lived through the fell winter. Everyone here has been tested through trials of blood and war, and come out stronger than ever. We are honorable men and women, but we are not like the south; we must face every threat with courage. The name of Badelgard must be feared by every people and nation, so that none will dare try to take our lands again!"

At her words the crowd erupted into cheers. Then, they began shouting the same chant as before: "All hail Queen Alysse! All hail Queen Alysse!"

"This is what I wished to say: the time of the Wardens is over!" Alysse shouted above them. "Go rebuild the nation! Make our farmlands productive, and our iron mines abundant! The Golden House will be rebuilt in its own time! We are all kings!"

CHAPTER SEVEN

That night, from the comfort of the Riverhall guesthouse, the sounds of celebration reached her ears. Again she huddled by the fire, and again her brother and father had pulled up a seat beside it. She had no concept of how long the winter had lasted. The nightmare had begun for her when rumors of the darklings spread, on that dark night when Andarr's Port was attacked. She had lost Harald; she had lost Brand. She had lost her child. She had lost the Golden House, but she had gained the throne.

"I am so proud of you," Ergould said.

She turned. The proud Duke Vis Voraigne was so old, yet so healthy. He could live another twenty years, and not surprise Alysse. His gray hair was a crown of wisdom. His purple, sable-lined robe was expensive, beyond the means of even the High King of Badelgard. But she knew he had earned it through wisdom, through ceaseless efforts of expansion and through wisdom and discretion.

"Thank you, father," she said.

"We will leave tomorrow," Ergould said. "But know this, my daughter: if ever you fall on hard times, if ever you are hungry or sick, you are welcome in our home and—when I die—in your brother's home. We have forgiven you. We understand, now, what you were fighting for. You will always be my daughter."

"Thank you, father." Alysse smiled. "I love you, and I love you, Lourges."

Her brother smiled.

They talked well into the night. She fell asleep on the rug, by the fire.

It was dark when she awoke. Outside, the sounds of celebration had died away. The winds had picked up, and to her surprise, a light snow was falling. A dread she had not felt for many days and hours returned in an instant. A lump formed in her throat. She stood up, rigid and cold.

She took a few steps to the door of the guesthouse. It hung slightly ajar. She caught a glimpse of a shadow, of a silhouette, outside. She braced herself and drew in a cold gasp, and then opened it.

A creature like a woman stood in the swirling snow. Her eyes were black and beady, buried in deep sockets. She knew—somehow—that this was the Great Mother, the goddess of the Ulfr.

Immediately, Alysse went rigid. Her heart pounded. She thought of retreating back through the door, but changed her mind. She would be the ultimate hypocrite if she backed down after the speech she had made. For too long, the lords and ladies of Badelgard had ignored the evil before them, fed it the souls of their children. She would not retreat. She stepped completely outside the door, and slammed it shut.

"What do you want?" Alysse shouted. "We have defeated you. Go away. You are not wanted here."

She bared her twisted yellow teeth. "I have come to bid you farewell. I see I am unwelcome."

"You are right."

The crone snarled. "I come, Alysse Riverhall, to make one last offer. I could make your people conquerors, a great nation that will rule the world. I could give your people power untold, an invincible strength that will lead to your domination of the south, and a boundless treasure hoard. Before I fade into the gray lands where the rest of my sisters lie, I wish to make one last offer…"

Alysse shook her head. There was no chance this would happen. Still, she asked, "And what would we do in exchange?"

"You would build me a temple in Oskir. Every year, you would offer me one of your firstborn. You would paint my insignia on your shields and conquer in my name."

Alysse laughed. "No. Never. Go away, demon! Go away! Go to the gray lands where your sisters lie…"

Her face contorted to a snarl, her claws grew to the length of sword-blades, her eyes burned like twin suns, and her body burst into a mass of mouths and wriggling tentacles; then, in a second's span, she was gone, and the snow turned to rain.

CHAPTER EIGHT

Alysse bade her brother and father a tearful goodbye. She waited at the gate while they rode off on horses with the other Zarubes. The sun was dawning, spreading warmth over the snowless grass. The sky was clear and bright blue. The water gushed down King's Falls, plummeting down into the river below. It was a new beginning.

In the city of Oskir, the tinkering of the blacksmith echoed through the morning air. In the streets, children played. The sounds of the lute and singing voices echoed from the mead hall. Even *The Lily House* appeared to return to its seedy business. The morning was warm and full of promise.

A flock of birds passed overhead. Things had returned to normal, but they would never be the same. Badelgard was irreparably changed. Oskir's population had dwindled by half, if not more. She had no crown to wear. Her queenly robe was a tattered green dress. Her palace was a blackened foundation. But Badelgard was saved. The evil, once merely hidden and appeased, was now vanquished.

She began walking toward the Riverhall guesthouse, where her temporary throne lay. In time the Golden House would be rebuilt, but for now there were more pressing concerns. The people of Badelgard had to regain their footing, reclaim their fields and pastures, before they could worry about the luxury of a privileged few.

A few—not one, she realized with a smile as Forni and Jarni came running up to her. The former Dragonpriests now wore coarse brown tunics: not the attire of princes, but it suited their roles better than the shirtless attire of before.

Forni embraced her. She had a lot of effort ahead of her: she had never known her children. But that was fine: she had a lot of time. She had a lot of time to spend with them.

She embraced Jarni next. The low-town was not as busy as it was, but the air was warm and a new life had infused it. Everything was new.

Harald had died fighting the possessed King Sven. Brand had

died at the gallows. Her two loves were gone. She doubted she would ever remarry. But she was High Queen of Badelgard.

She turned and gazed into the rising sun. The Great Witch—risen from her ancient barrow—was no more, and her strange goddess had passed away from the realm of men.

As the sunbeams hit her full-on, she grabbed her two boys and laughed. Her life was ahead of her. Badelgard had been made new. The world was at their fingertips. She laughed again. The church bells of Vana began to ring, and in heaven surely the valkyries were dancing and singing a new song.

All was new. All was new.

Once more it began to rain. All was new.

The fell winter was over. The bells resounded, banishing all despair.

She laughed. She hugged her children tighter than ever, and let the sun bathe her as she cried. All was new. The fell winter was over.

THE END

EPILOGUE

An excerpt from *The Annals of the Kings of Badelgard*:

Queen Alysse Riverhall reigned over the land with wisdom and mercy for many years. Forni took ill and passed on peacefully to Altgard.

In the wake of his brother's death, Jarni Riverhall assumed the throne. He married—against the laws of the Wardens, but with his mother's approval—a woman that in past epochs would have been considered 'lowly born.'

Alysse lived to old age and passed away peacefully on her deathbed in the rebuilt Golden House. From Jarni Riverhall on, a line of wise and just kings reigned over Badelgard. From the time of Jarni to the present era, the kings led the wars and raids and conquests at the vanguard. And from the conquests and raids of the Riverhall kings, wealth untold passed into the coffers of Oskir and the other towns. Thus began a golden age, but the fell winter was never forgotten, and the people were forever thankful for the brave deeds of their forebears. Never again did the Ulfr arise, from then until the present day; a wild forest grew in the place of the Ice Shelf. The Seat of the Great Mother, now turned to a pile of stones, was just that. No trace of the Ulfr evil has remained, and the name of Alysse Riverhall is honored to this day.

GLOSSARY

A note on dates: All dates are reckoned by the Imperial system. In 1 Y.E. (Year of the Empire) the first brick of Peregoth was laid, while Y.B.E. (Year Before the Empire) marks dates prior to that event.

A note on Zarube names:

Vis = "Of" in the familial sense, especially when prefacing the name of a noble house.

Diu = Indicates a son or daughter.

Altgard: See *Hall of the Slain.*

Buntringer: The ancestor of the Badelgard people. His sons were Hjarta, Himnall, and Helgur, from whom the human population of Badelgard descends.

Dragonmount, the: A tall peak in the northeast of Badelgard where the Green Dragon once slumbered. The ancient Ulfr believed it was haunted and knew that a great beast slept there, but dared not disturb it.

Garrone: A small county in Zarubain ruled by the House Sargonnais.

Great Witch, the: The highest Ulfr title, representing the pinnacle of magical power.

Green Dragon, the: The dragon, named Skruga, who allied with the Badelgard humans and destroyed the ancient Ulfr with fire. He is believed to be the last dragon to leave for the west.

Green Dragons: The priesthood of Skruga residing in a stone temple at the base of the Dragonmount.

Hall of the Slain: Also known as Altgard, this is the place where Vana, goddess of victory, and her valkyries are supposed to reside. It is believed to be a spacious longhouse in a mountain meadow within the broader realm of heaven. Only skilled warriors and men of great honor are chosen to live in the presence of Lady

Vana and her warrior-maidens. By day, the risen dead fight, but at night, they recover from any wounds they received during the day and feast until the early hours of the morning in the presence of the valkyries.

Healing House, the: The most highly respected center of healing and medicine in Badelgard. Located in Trowfell Keep, the large complex contains steam baths, a vast collection of imported herbs and assorted herbal remedies, and a small library of medicinal texts. A large staff of healers and physicians—associated with the religious order of Vana—attends to the sick and injured.

Housecarl: An order of protectors for the various noble houses. Housecarls are considered highborn and are required to defend their lieges to the death if need be. Appointment to housecarl is the only way a lowborn can enter the nobility. A housecarl can be stripped of his rank easily; all it requires is the liege-lord's verbal pronouncement. The order is open to both men and women.

King's Drawbridge, the: An enormous wooden drawbridge that can only be lowered via the High King's command. It is the only way, excluding sea travel, that a person can enter the low-lying southern lands. In winter, it is Badelgard's sole exit. High King Sven has not lowered it since the beginning of his reign.

Marabelle: The goddess of horses. Called Eliane in Badelgard.

Marabelle, Knights of: A Zarube knightly order and cult, serving the House of Voraigne.

Morguis: A form of undead, considered the pinnacle creation of the Ulfr. Through a combination of alchemical and magical processes, the necromancer creator gave superior intelligence, strength, and size to a maggot. The specimen was then placed within a corpse. These specimens—first created in the 200s Y.B.E.—were initially met with disgust and horror. However, the Ulfr queen eventually sanctioned their production and used them to kill dissidents. Despite their new acceptance, morguises eventually gained a reputation for pride and disobedience, and would often break free of their creators and go on widespread killing sprees. Despite this, their production continued until the Ulfr destruction circa 300 Y.E.

Nobility: The nobility of Badelgard is called highborn and expected to rule above the common, or lowborn. At heart they are a warrior class, and in their inception expected to protect the kingdom and shy away from any temptations of luxury or excess. The top tier of the nobility consists of the earls, who rule great towns and citadels across Badelgard. Below earls are the barons. Only one baronial family owns land and rules its own city: the Riverhalls of Andarr's Port. The other barons rule petty villages. The Osters, an earl family, took the High Throne after the Accession Crisis of 656 and changed the name of the capital from Rigthorp to Oskir.

Skruga: See *Green Dragon*.

Sky Cliffs, the: A sheer precipice separating Badelgard from the low-lying southern lands. They stretch approximately 2,000 feet and can only be descended via the King's Drawbridge.

Somergard: The land of the House Summerleaf.

Sorelden: See Ulfr.

Summerleaf, House of: A Badelgard highborn family.

Troll: A large, hulking creation of Ulfr wizards.

Ulfr: A human term for the people that originally inhabited Badelgard. The Ulfr called themselves the Sorelden, and called their land Sorelda. As a people, the Ulfr had many customs that the human invaders thought to be odd or even evil. They suffered the effects of severe inbreeding due to widespread brother-sister marriages, which caused a number of physical deformities: instead of five toes, most Sorelden had two large toes; only three fingers and a thumb on each hand; and yellow eyes. They worshiped a deity called The Great Mother whom the invading humans identified as a demon. Each year, there was a lottery and those Ulfr families who were picked had to sacrifice one of their children to The

Great Mother. Despite their deformities, the Ulfr were powerful wizards and most of them—perhaps because of their worship of the death-loving Great Mother—had the gift of necromancy. With their sorcery, they created trolls: hulking beasts which served them in war. Although the Ulfr were intelligent, rigid adherence to tradition created a refusal to innovate. Hiding on a steely peak was what the Ulfr called The Slumbering Beast—a green-scaled dragon—who soon allied with the invading humans and rained fire down upon their cities and temples. The Sorelden were all gone circa 300 Y.E., not to be seen again for five hundred years... until the current Ulfr Crisis (circa 825 Y.E.).

Valkyries: The warrior-maidens who serve Vana and scour Badelgard for worthy additions to the Hall of the Slain. They are portrayed as beautiful, winged women holding spears.

Vana: The goddess of victory and the home. She is portrayed in art as a big-boned, brown-haired woman in a white robe, often plucking her trademark instrument, the harp. She is the original patron goddess of the Badelgard humans; the other deity whom they worship, the Green Dragon, was added to the pantheon after the conquest.

Voraigne, House of: One of the most ancient noble houses of Zarubain. It controls a duchy of the same name located very close to the royal estate. The Voraignes are one of the kingdom's most highly-respected families.

Waterwood, the: A marshy forest in the west of Badelgard.

Woodhome: A hunting lodge and general base of operations for the Riverhall Order of Scouts.

White Wolves: A species of Great Wolves with snow-white coats, pink eyes, and viciously territorial tendencies. In winter, they can often be seen rolling in the snow or bounding through the mountains in a never-ending hunt. White Wolf Keep, residence of the Silverback noble family, is named after them.

Zarubad: A city of about 200,000 people. The capital of Zarubain.

Zarubain: A nation south of Badelgard.

ABOUT THE AUTHOR

Cursed at birth with a wild imagination, Andrew Cooper spent his youth dreaming of worlds more exciting than Earth.

He is a graduate of the Odyssey Writing Workshop. His stories have appeared in Morpheus Tales, Fear and Trembling, Residential Aliens and Mindflights, among others.

CONTACT THE AUTHOR

Visit **www.aj-cooper.com** to sign up for the newsletter and stay up-to-date on new releases.

Find him on Facebook at:

www.facebook.com/AJCooperauthor

Enchanted Forest is a short story series available on any e-reader or computer. The first two episodes follow...

KALAMAR: A SHORT GUIDE

The Kalamar Forest and the adjacent Murk Swamps lie in a place where the material world (VARDA) and the faerie world (AVENDA) converge. Amid the invasive vegetation and predatory species, the norgs—descendants of dwarvish settlers—have staked out a life for themselves.

CHIEF TOWNS

The king rules the forest from his fortress at Bayne's Dain. Underneath him are the Magisters of the chief towns: namely, Goldborough, Honeymead Village, Duskville, and Aureleum.
• Goldborough serves as chief town of Goldenwood, a region of productive apple orchards.
• Honeymead, the largest settlement of Kalamar, serves as chief town of Summervine.
• Duskville is a frontier town bordering the edge of the Cobwood, a dangerous place filled with Giant Spiders. Among the smallest settlements in Kalamar, most of its population is composed of norgish warriors on duty.
• Aureleum serves as chief town of Greenacre, a region of productive farmland. It lies outside of the fey line.

GEOGRAPHY

The Kalamar Forest lies between the Great Wall to the north—impenetrable and towering in size—and the barren heath-land to the south. To the west, across the Great River, lie the Murk Swamps, a region filled with harpies, as well as the legendary Mandragora (a carnivorous, mobile plant) and other terrible dangers. To the east is Greenacre, the norgish farmland.

HISTORY

After the fall of the ancient dwarven kingdoms in the Shadow War, the dwarf-lord Bayne and a group of his followers fled the forces of darkness. They crossed the Great Western Mountains—what many thought was an impossible feat—and many perished in the journey. In 316 YBE, they reached Kalamar. Bayne decided to settle here, and made war on the harpies of the forest, overcoming them by 315 and driving them into the swamps. He built a fortress in the dwarfish style, naming it DAIN BAYNU ("Bayne's Fortress.")

Bayne renamed his race the norgs. They settled sporadically through the enchanted forest. A further Norg-Harpy War from 315 to 313 YBE led to the creation of a peace treaty between the two races.

Enchanted Forest takes place 300 years later, in the first century YE.

SIGHTS

The Lonely Inn: Kalamar's oldest and most famous inn, lying in the exact middle of the road between Goldborough and Duskville. Established in 320 YE, shortly after the Norg-Harpy War, it has stood ever since. Featuring many deer head and moose head trophies and a warm, spacious hearth, it is a destination all by itself. In addition to food fit for any gourmand, it features hot baths for the weary traveler and homey décor.

The Sheeh: Considered the forest's heart, this kernel of fey power has never been fully explored. Firvalg (lupine creatures), bound by an ancient spell of entrapment, hunt the living within its dense vegetation. Few that enter the Sheeh return alive.

Valley of Kings: The resting place of the ancient norg-lords.

HAG HOLLOW

THE FIRST EPISODE OF *ENCHANTED FOREST*

Piorin stretched his arms toward the top of the bed, but he couldn't reach it. His nanny grabbed his tiny hand and hoisted him up onto the soft, cold linen.

"I will never be a warrior," Piorin said. "I'm too small."

"Maybe one day you'll be big and strong; sometimes, norgs grow in spurts." His nanny smiled widely. "You may become a brave warrior yet. And you will be a wise warrior; you will remember to always bring your sword and pony wherever you go."

Piorin giggled.

"Don't laugh," the nanny said and ran a hand through his brown hair. "There are things out there who eat norgs. And whatever you do, never go into the western swamps. In them are snakes and harpies. But worst of all, there are hags who will gobble you up."

Piorin loved his nanny's stories, but even as a child he did not believe in hags. And besides, as a member of the House of Bayne—the most ancient and powerful clan in the Kalamar Forest—his parents expected absolute bravery out of him.

When his nanny went missing on Piorin's thirteenth birthday, he mourned in private. His father Filosha already looked down on him for his tiny size, and his mother Branwyn thought him too emotional. He cried into his bed—the bed where his nanny told him her stories.

When Piorin reached puberty, and he hardly grew at all, he received the unfortunate nickname of Shortsprout—which followed him everywhere he went, and even the scullery-maids and servants used it against him. His parents, who wanted a powerful warrior as a son, seemed the most disappointed in his stature. All this made him miss his nanny all the more.

Still, the traditional ceremony took place when Piorin turned seventeen. In a small clearing in the wood, the servants lit torches. The dancers performed a pavane to the sound of pipes and drums. The partygoers ate a feast of venison and hard cider. Pink and blue ribbons draped from the trees, and the norg-children danced around maypoles.

At sundown, Piorin waited in the center of the clearing. His father walked up to him and handed him a sword. The clan blacksmith had named it Elvathan: "Death to Enemies." The clan sorceress had dipped it in eldritch waters while hot, and woven the blade with intricate magic: spells of ivy and scrub-brush and green growth; spells of harsh sunlight and pricking thorns and choking vines. The clan priest named him Pirosha—"sha" being a title equivalent to the human "sir"—and his father brought him a handsome silver pony, which Pirosha named "Luna," or, in their language, "Light."

"You are a man now," said his father, whose beard by now had turned gray. "Serve me well. You will lead armies against the spiders and the harpies. You have trained all your childhood with the sword; now you have one of your own. You have no brothers or sisters; you are the only one who survived to adulthood. Therefore, you must carry on your mother's and my lineage."

Pirosha nodded.

Eirin, high priest of the earth-god Peong, stepped forward as his father turned and walked back. "It is an honor to die in battle," he recited. "But it is a greater honor to live in victory. Remember this throughout all the wars you wage, all the lands you conquer, all the innocents you save."

Piorin knew the speech was only ceremonial; norgs no longer fought each other, nor did anyone die in battle. The House of Bayne already conquered the whole forest.

The priest continued the rehearsed, ceremonial speech that had not changed since its inception. "When Lord Bayne crossed the great snowy mountains and wandered to this land, we drove the harpies from the forest and into the western swamps. When the Big People from the south tried to conquer us, we made a treaty. Once the people called us dwarves; now, that is improper, for we do not live under earth nor do we create great works of iron. We are thin, and we shave our beards. We are the norgs, the dwarves of the forest. Remember this always."

"I will," said Pirosha.

That autumn, when the lush green oaks turned to shades of red and orange and brown, and the air turned chilly, Pirosha's father grew ill. At the same time, rumors spread that strangers had entered the Kalamar Forest. There were rumors in Lockland, the land-between-two-streams, that a Gray Ghost wandered the woods, singing a captivating song and drawing people out of their homes that were never seen again. Some said a dark spirit had possessed the lord of Honeymead Village, who had fallen into a delirious state and given mad orders. And when Pirosha heard the Gray Ghost singing in Bayne's Dain—the chief province of Kalamar—he decided to act. He fetched his pony from the stables, got his sword, and was just about to leave through the gate when his father's bodyguard stopped him.

"Your father wishes to speak with you," they said.

Pirosha grudgingly obeyed, going into the stone-hewn fortress where he and his family lived.

Lord Filosha slumped lifelessly in his throne, yet he still spoke. "Do not leave, my son," he said. "Do not go into the forest and chase after the Gray Ghost."

"Why not?" said Pirosha.

"Because I said so. Is that not adequate reason, shortsprout?"

The name hurt him and was unlike his father, but he dared not question him. "I suppose it is, milord," said Pirosha. "But I do not understand."

"You need not understand," said Filosha. "Only know that it is against my wishes for you to fight the Gray Ghost."

"Father," Pirosha said, "how did you know that's where I was going?"

Filosha flashed a yellow smile. "I know many things, young Pirosha, that you will not begin to imagine."

Pirosha shivered. His father seemed not himself.

That night, a captivating voice filled the forest. Pirosha listened from his bedside window.

Come to me, and dance, and sing
Come to me and honor your king
We bask in joy, and you should follow
For a male has been born in the Hollow!

Pirosha tried to make sense out of the song, but it was futile. Pirosha never heard the song in his life, and his court minstrel knew hundreds of songs. The ethereal voice only caused the garden-snake of unease to wriggle in his stomach.

After a little effort, he fell asleep.

~

In the morning, Pirosha heard that a mother and two children had wandered off into the forest that night, northeastward into the wilds toward Summervine, and not returned. He determined at that moment that he had to disobey his father, or he would not be serving his first priority: the realm itself. He slipped into the forest and evaded the guards.

Into the oaks, he rode on his pony Luna: deep into the chilly, red-gold forest in the cold light of dawn. He had to get to the bottom of the song, and the mystery of the errant Gray Ghost.

He rode the pony northeast as fast as it would take him. About two miles in, the scent of something cooking hit his nose. It was a foul, rancid smell. He followed it fast and drew his sword, and at last came to a forest clearing. There, a cauldron boiled above a burning fire. Next to it was a woman in a gray cowl, humming as she stirred the pot. She was huge—the size of one of the Big People, if not taller. She began sniffing.

"I smell the flesh of a norg," she said. "His musk is royal. Granny Nightshade might gobble you up, but she will cook you well. And you will be ground-up and served as mash to the holy gullet of newborn Lord Milkweed. What greater honor is there in all Varda?"

Pirosha drew his sword quietly out of its eelskin sheath. Then he raised it above his head, and prepared to charge.

It was then that Pirosha realized Granny Nightshade had, instead of nails, long claws that extended from her fingers—razor-sharp claws that looked like they could tear the skin off a norg's bones. He couldn't see her face, and he didn't want to.

Pirosha charged as his heart thundered inside his chest. At last he was within striking distance of Nightshade; he hacked downward with his sword—and her claws, hard as steel, blocked effectively. Then she pushed him hard, sending him flying off the pony. He hit the ground with a painful thud.

"Ah, I can see you now," said Nightshade. "You are small, even among the norgs. Making mash out of you wouldn't satisfy Lord Milkweed; he is a hungry baby and craves much raw flesh."

Pirosha stood up. Despite his fear, a growl escaped him; he didn't mind norgs calling him small, but a witch? He charged again; with one swipe of her claws, she cut his arm.

"You are brave. You would have made a good warrior. Too bad today is your death-day."

"How do you know that?" Pirosha said.

Nightshade let out a squawking, gooselike laugh. She grabbed the folds of her cowl. "Because no norg can handle the wondrous nature of my appearance."

"Try me!"

The cowl dropped. Pirosha's heart went up into his throat. She was naked; her skin was wrinkled and bluish-purple. Her breasts were small and disfigured. Her eyes—her eyes!—they bulged, mismatched in size: bloodshot, yet deathly hungry for flesh. Moles, warts and boils covered her sharp, jutting face; and yellow teeth were thin as needles and twisted.

Pirosha screamed and shielded his eyes, falling onto the floor. The blood from his arm collected around him. If he had looked at her for more than one second, his heart would have ruptured. "Never have I seen such ugliness!" Pirosha screamed.

Granny Nightshade laughed bashfully. "Oh. Thank you."

"You will haunt my dreams forever."

"You shouldn't flatter me so!" she said. "I could force you to look at me for longer… then you would die. But I won't do it. Do you know why?"

"No."

"Because I like you, young norg. You are bolder and stronger than any norg I've met. You are much stronger than your father, whom I possessed…"

"What do you want from us? Why did you come?"

"The child, Milkweed, has been born," said Nightshade. "I have crossed the border to announce it. He is Hag-Odam, the one who will lead our race to dominate Kalamar. When he is grown, all my coven will come. We will hack and burn the forest, and reshape it into our image. My deed is done; I have announced Milkweed's birth to all; and I will return in seven years, when the holy child has come of age. If you wish… pay your respects in Hag Hollow."

She vanished, flying away in the pot on wings of shadow.

When Pirosha returned to Bayne's Dain, the clan physician bound his wounds, yet they could not heal the memory of the uncloaked Nightshade.

As he wrapped the bandage tight, the physician said without much regret, "Your father died this morning."

Pirosha went to his bedroom. He shut the door as hot tears streaked from his eyes. He would never get the chance to prove his worth to old Filosha. He would never get the chance to win his father's respect and love. The hag had sent him plummeting into death.

At the funeral the next day, Pirosha's wellspring of tears had run dry. But a fire kindled in him. He would avenge his father. He would go into Hag Hollow, into the swamps, and he would slay the queen hag. Either that, or he would die trying.

The next day, he went to the clan sorceress. She outfitted him with charms: a pentacle to ground him in the earth; a steel Cerne's Cross for the blessing of nature; a star amulet to protect him from the Hag's Eye; and a dozen rings to grant him the sorceress's protection. She performed a ritual of smoke and incense, read him wise sayings from the Book of Earth, and anointed him with oil.

Piorin left the estate in the care of his mother. Then, once the magic was finished, he hopped on his pony and rode west... west into the forbidden swamps, the land his nanny told him never to visit.

At the eaves of the Murk Swamps, he hesitated. Harpies lived in the swamps: hideous, winged creatures and masters of poison. Yet when Pirosha's ancestor, Lord Bayne, defeated them, they made a truce: norgs could go into the swamps without incident, as long as they didn't make trouble. Killing a norg without good reason would be an act of war. Yet often those who went into the swamp never returned, though no war had waged between the harpies and the norgs for a hundred years.

Still, Pirosha forced himself to enter into the thick, watery growth. He crossed the bridge into the river and reached an overused, hole-covered path. He cut through thick, thorny growth and entered the swamp. Above him hung a canopy so thick that Pirosha felt he walked from day into night.

Here he would inquire for directions to Hag Hollow.

The first "village" he came to in the dark recesses was a collection of huts from which smoke and the scent of roasting crawfish floated out. The walls of the huts were made of clay and sticks; the roofs, dried yellow reeds. Signs hung above some of the huts, which Pirosha couldn't read although they were in Dwarf script, and read like a conglomeration of hissing noises; the harpies had no writing system of their own prior to contact with the dwarves.

Feeling his heart race as the harpies moved toward him—the raven-winged, predatory females and the wingless, scrawny males—Pirosha touched the hilt of his sword. Met with sharp hisses, he removed his grasp. "Hello," he said. "Do any of you speak Dwarvish?"

"Me do," a black-haired harpy woman said in a thick, spitting accent. "I am Mina. I am wise-woman of Mugrat Village. Only wise-woman in leagues."

"I inquire for directions to Hag Hollow."

A few harpies gasped. Then, dead silence.

"You look smarter than you talk," said Mina. "Hags are ravenous. Hags have been robbing children of ours. Eating them in their swaddling clothes. No one help us harpies. Hag Hollow is deadly. You will not survive, not with the most amulets in the world. Not clothed in the sun, not clothed in the stars. Male-hag has been born; a feeding frenzy has started to feed him. Bad times. Dark times."

"I repeat myself," said Pirosha. "I inquire for directions to Hag Hollow."

"Fool, you are," said Mina. "We harpies do not care whether you live or die. However, if you are eaten, one of us will not be. I will lead you to Buckwort Village. Hag Hollow is four leagues up Barkflower Path, and one short walk west into the swamp. We call the hollow Heart of Darkness because it is a source of all evil." She paused. "I will lead you to Buckwort. I see you are brave. Even the harpies honor that. I hear in your part of world… the males are warriors. Queer… I never heard of such things. But I will lead you, brave-male."

"Thank you, Mina," Pirosha said.

They ate a full meal of barely-cooked crawfish. Then, after grabbing a crude iron knife, a sling, and a few stones, Mina took off down the path and Pirosha followed her on his pony.

They rode on. They passed through the muddy, overgrown bog and Pirosha occasionally thought of taking some of the large pink or orange swamp-flowers to brighten his day; however, Mina told him they were "deadly poisonous."

As he rode poor Luna, Pirosha wondered at how a harpy was helping one of the norgs. None of the norgs back home would believe it. But there was a saying attributed to Lord Bayne: "Nothing brings two together like a mutual enemy," referring to the First War.

At dusk, they came to Buckwort Village. Mina shrieked. Pirosha looked ahead. The entire village seemed to have sunk below the muck; the dozen huts were half-submerged, as if someone or something had drawn them into the mud with a spell. Skeletons—picked clean of meat—floated in the water.

"Tiacka save us!" Mina cried.

A whimper escaped Pirosha, and suddenly the amulets hanging around his neck felt heavy as millstones.

"The hag-baby will eat us all!" Mina howled.

"Hush! Hush!" Pirosha said. "You'll draw attention to us."

"Sorry," she whispered. "This is the biggest city I know. All dead! All dead! The great wise-woman Hiskwort taught me here. She is sure dead." She turned to Pirosha, cheeks streaked with tears. She shrieked again.

"Hush!" Pirosha growled. "Someone will hear you."

But she kept sobbing loudly. Something green began to rise out of the water.

Pirosha took off on the northward-leading path and galloped away as Mina's agonizing death-cries filled the swamp. Guilt seized Pirosha, yet he knew that if he stayed back to protect Mina they would both die and the hags would never be stopped.

As he rode up the path, hands shaking, he shut his eyes and prayed that Peong would grant him protection.

Pirosha knew that sleeping was a terrible idea. He rode up Barkflower Path as night fell. As the swamp grew pitch-black and completely unnavigable to norg eyes, Pirosha realized he had not brought torch.

What a fool I am!

Then lights appeared all around, granting dim illumination. It became evident that the orange swamp flowers had begun to glow. Eventually Pirosha's eyes adjusted and once more, the land became visible. He took a few deep breaths, then coaxed Luna on.

At the marking Mina described, he hopped off Luna. He did not want anything to happen to her; to Pirosha, animals were always innocent and using them for warfare was always cruel. He brushed her mane, and bade her a quiet night and to run off.

He hesitated. After ten seconds of waiting, he took a trembling step into the thicket. He felt eyes watching him at all corners, but he knew it was just his imagination. At least, he told himself he knew. As he walked westward—west toward the long-set sun—he prayed without cease, eyes nevertheless open. He drew his sword out quietly. He made sure not to step into any noisy pools or crunching leaves; hags could not see very well, but they had a much better sense of hearing than norgs or even the Big People—especially the Big People.

As he made his way through the tangled brush, torchlights appeared in the distance. He crept toward them as silently as he could. Then something in the water caught his eye: green, yet a lighter color green than any plant he had ever seen. He looked down, observing in the dim light, and saw it was not a plant but something bigger.

It was the size of one of the Big People, wrinkled and green. It was a creature—a woman!—with algae for hair and needle-thin teeth, shut eyes and folded hands. It was a Sea Hag, a hideous lady of the water, and if Pirosha made a single movement, she would sense him and drag him under.

Trembling cold seized him. He shut his eyes and waited, praying to the dear gods that she wouldn't smell him—after all, she was under water—or that he wouldn't move and she, sense the tremor of his step.

When he opened his eyes, she had floated by. Pirosha swallowed his fear and walked toward the illumination. He prayed every second that he would not run into another Sea Hag, floating in the swamp and waiting for a meal to snatch. When his nanny had warned him not to wander beside lakes as a child because of Sea Hags, he hadn't believed her. Now, he did.

At last he came to Hag Hollow. For once Pirosha could see the night sky and the billions of stars. Hags of all kinds, much taller than Pirosha, had joined hands in a circle and were dancing as they sang a song in their grating voices:

A child was born on Midsummer's Day
A male child, a hag-child—Lord Milkweed, I say!
His eyes are bright scarlet, he's hungry for bread
Bread made of crushed-bones! From the best bones he's fed!

Every variety of hag Pirosha knew danced in the circle: the gray Death Hags who fed on life force, who appeared when a person was about to die; the purple Night Hags whose ugliness could kill (thank Peong, Pirosha did not look at them closely); the green Sea Hags; the blue Dream Hags who appeared in nightmares; the white-and-red Pox Hags who caused ravaging disease; and many more, of other colors, that Pirosha did not recognize.

At the center of the circle lay a green baby with bloodshot eyes, gnawing a bone in his already-grown teeth. A pile of bones sat at his feet.

If he had not been green-colored, and a norg-eater, Pirosha would have considered Lord Milkweed the most beautiful baby in existence. Pirosha's nanny had told him hag males were as beautiful as their mother and lovers were hideous. Their powers of magic vastly exceeded any other of the hags; yet they only lived to age 33.

Despite his efforts at silence, a whimper escaped Pirosha. He hesitated again, then took an awkward step forward toward the muck… and a coarse hand caught him by the scruff of his collar.

"Hello, Pirosha," said the voice of Granny Nightshade.

Nightshade brought Pirosha into the center of the dance circle, right next to Lord Milkweed. Pirosha shielded his eyes so that he could not view the death-inducing ugliness of Nightshade.

"Why must you be so evil?" he said. "Why must you eat, and eat, and eat? I came here to defeat you, but now I know that it is impossible. You Big People are far too strong for me… I am little even for a norg." A hot tear streaked down Pirosha's cheek.

"Hush, hush now," Nightshade said like a mother to her child. She cradled him in his arms, which sent a fiery streak of anger through Pirosha's body.

Pirosha clenched his teeth and made an effort to channel his rage. He grabbed Nightshade's neck and tried to squeeze, to either strangle her or die in the effort. It was no use; her neck was thick as bone.

Pirosha sighed in frustration. "My nanny was right! I should never have gone into the swamp."

"Yes, your nanny was right," Nightshade said. "So why did you disobey her?"

"I disobeyed her because you hags threaten to end our lives in Kalamar. You killed my father… you kill, kill, kill! Eat, eat, eat!"

"You are brave," Nightshade said. "You will go down in history as the bravest norg who ever lived. You will have many adventures in your lifetime."

"What are you talking about? This will surely be my last adventure!" Pirosha said. "And so be it! I will die knowing that I tried to stop you."

The hags kept dancing round the green baby.

"There are things out there that think of children as snacks," Nightshade said. "And whatever you do, don't go into the western swamps, for in them lies death."

"Wait!" Pirosha said. "My nanny said that! So long ago I'm surprised I can remember. And you—were you watching me my entire childhood?"

"Not watching," Nightshade said with a knowing smile, and Pirosha grew angrier. "Know that it is I who birthed Lord Milkweed. The spirit of nature chose me out of all my sisters. I will not harm you,

Pirosha. I do not plan on it. I, Nightshade—high mother of the Murk Coven, second only to Granny Yaga in power—will not let you come to harm tonight."

"I will kill you or die trying!"

"You may try!" Nightshade said. "But you won't, and you can't, nor will you die trying. Tonight was the greatest test of your bravery. I will not let Kalamar come to harm. I will be your guidance. I wanted to test your mettle. And you have proven yourself brave! Brave enough to come into the swamps where your nanny told you not to. Brave enough to face Hag Hollow."

"Did you kill my nanny?"

"No," Nightshade said. "She and I are the same; I was, and still am, your nanny."

"Liar!"

"I disguised myself in the form of a norg; I was sickeningly beautiful in that form. By your father's seed I grew pregnant; I lay pregnant for three years; young Milkweed clawed inside me ceaselessly."

"You killed my father."

"Only so that you would be rightful Lord of Kalamar."

"I didn't ask to be Lord of Kalamar."

"It is your destiny."

The hags sang a little louder.

Pirosha grabbed his pentacle and cried out, "I call upon you, Lord Peong, to protect me!"

Nightshade grabbed all his amulets, tore them from his neck, and cast them to the floor. "Do not try to use magic against your nanny!"

"You are not my nanny."

"I am. And when you need my guidance—and you *will* need it in the troubles ahead—come only to Hag Hollow and know that I will not let my sisters eat you. Nor my son, and your brother, blessed Milkweed."

"You killed all those harpies!"

"When we have satisfied Milkweed's craving for raw flesh, we will stop the killing," Nightshade said. "Until then, it is nothing less than necessary." She paused. "Are you ready to return to the place of your birth? The killing is done in Kalamar; no more norgs will be harmed. You will be safe, but only for a while. Trouble will fall upon the land, and it will not be borne of hags, but by those you call the Big People."

It dawned on Pirosha that he could not defeat Nightshade. If he could not beat her, he may as well accept her mercy. "So be it!" Pirosha cried. "Take me back to Kalamar, my home. I cannot imagine having a more frightening nanny…"

"It lies on you to protect Kalamar from the Big People."

"So be it, nanny… and…"

He hesitated and looked at the green baby, gnawing on a bone.

"Brother. Nanny Nightshade… and Brother Milkweed," Pirosha finally said, before the hag queen spirited him off in the wings of the night and delivered him onto his father's bed.

BIG BLACK DOG

THE SECOND EPISODE OF *ENCHANTED FOREST*

I.

Pirosha Shortsprout galloped down the weathered trails on his pony Luna. A message of distress had called him to the province known as the Sheeh; and he rode alone. A single note, written on lambskin and delivered by night-riders, drew him here:

Help. Trouble in the Sheeh. Come quickly. –Lord Diarsha

The people of Pirosha's village, Bayne's Dain, called the Sheeh the heart of the forest. Uncultivated and untamed, Loxdon Village—its only settlement—lay on the northernmost edge. After an all-day ride down these twisting paths, he finally drew close. Here the thorns and bushes encroached on the path even though, by royal edict, they were trimmed every morning. The vegetation of the Sheeh respected no mortal boundaries.

Yet at last, the green tunnel opened up and, a few dozen yards distant, Loxdon Village appeared on the banks of the River Sheogan. Five thatched-roof buildings clustered around a tiny square. Three houses—if memory served—an inn and a grocer. Hardly a village, by anyone's standards.

Pirosha slowed his pace. Luna trotted over the small wooden bridge that spanned the River Sheogan. In the darkening sky, Pirosha looked up and saw no end to the towering hickories, and shivered.

"Here you are, at last." Lord Diarsha stood on the edge of the town square. An older norg, he had a set of thick gray hair. He wore an elaborately-woven brocade shirt with large black buttons. Numerous golden rings gleamed on his old fingers.

He dresses better than me, Pirosha thought, *and I am his king.* "How fares the Sheeh, Diarsha?"

Diarsha bowed. "Not good. A witch lives among us. By day she is a common norg… by night she summons a demon to terrorize us—a big black dog. Just last night, one of our village's finest norgs was killed by the beast."

"Are you sure this is wizardry?" Pirosha asked. "Magic is rare among norgs."

"It is not wizardry. It is devilry. The black dog has eyes of flame and we can hear its growling all night long." Diarsha's face went white. "It is—and forgive me for speaking of such things—a demon. The witch has made a pact with dark forces."

"Stranger things have been seen in the Sheeh."

"You are our last hope," Diarsha said. "Korin, our only warrior, did battle with the beast; and he is now dead."

"Perhaps it is just a dog… a creature from the Heart of the Sheeh."

"It is a witch," Diarsha said zealously. "And I know who it is."

"Who?"

"Her name is Imowyn. She doesn't socialize, and she keeps strange pets, and she collects books."

"None of those things mean she is a witch," Pirosha said. Yet he would talk to this Imowyn anyway.

Imowyn, Pirosha soon learned, lived in a closed-off room in the second story of one of the houses. She rarely came outside, according to her neighbors. When she did socialize, she spoke with strange enthusiasm about the herbs and fruits that grew in the Sheeh, and even though her neighbors made their disinterest obvious, she kept prattling on as if she didn't care.

Pirosha knocked on Imowyn's door. No one answered. He knocked again. No one answered. He tried the doorknob, but it was locked from the inside. He wondered if she were gone; and then a cat's meow sounded from inside, and a female voice said, "There, there, my dear. Don't be frightened of the stranger."

"Excuse me, miss!" Pirosha called out. "I mean no harm. Please open the door!"

But she never opened the door, and Pirosha in frustration left for the inn.

The Loxdon Inn had two stories, a large stone hearth, and a spacious main hall where, notably, no norgs reclined except Pirosha. The innkeeper brought him supper and Pirosha sat there, sipping at a mug of green-apple cider and nibbling at a hunk of white bread until Lord Diarsha arrived.

"So she wouldn't even open her door for the king, eh?" Diarsha said. "That's the word around town."

"I'm afraid not."

"Doesn't that sound suspicious to you?" Diarsha asked.

"I suppose. We must force her door open... place a warrant against her home."

"I have done that already," Diarsha said. "She has enchanted the wood so that it is hard as steel. No norg can break through it... not even with a hammer!"

"Does she ever leave?"

"Sometimes she leaves into the Heart of the Sheeh," Diarsha said. "She goes in so deep that no one can follow her. And sometimes we hear her singing... and once, just last week, little Nadin Glammer spotted the black dog in her lap."

A witch that enchants wood, and survives the treacherous Heart of the Sheeh. This was more trouble than Pirosha anticipated. He took a big sip of cider. "I suppose we need to follow her. We need to wait until she leaves her room." He paused, realizing the gravity of what he was about to say. "In the meantime, I require as many able-bodied norgs as you can muster. I will face the Black Dog tonight."

"You can't be serious," Diarsha said. "The beast is dangerous. I don't want to see any norgs die tonight. Our town is small enough, and if even a few die, it'll be the end of Loxdon Village as we know it."

"Fine. Then I'll face him alone."

Diarsha gasped. "Gods, no! Though you are short, you are my king; and I cannot let your lordship die."

"It will not be your fault if I die. It will be my own." Pirosha stood up from his chair. He needed to make preparations; and besides, only a drop remained of his cider. The Black Dog that haunted Loxdon Village lurked outside.

Darkness crept over the sky. Thanks to the thick wall of thorns and vines that surrounded the village, Pirosha could barely see at all. But in the center of the town square, torches granted dim illumination. Vines coiled around them as if the Sheeh wished to devour the village whole.

Pirosha drew his sword. He drew out his sword, Elvathan. His stomach wound in knots as he stood there, waiting for the Black Dog's growl. As the sky darkened and the stars revealed themselves, the autumn air grew chill. Pirosha shivered in the cold and wished for warmer clothing.

"Father Peong, Lord of Earth and Stone," he recited, "protect me from the cutting-scythe that strives to take my vine of life."

Lights appeared in the shadow beyond the torches. Two pinpoints of yellow: Eyes. A growl started—soft at first, but then so deafening that the ground seemed to quiver beneath Pirosha's feet.

Pirosha eyed the inn door, thinking he still had a chance to run in. But a good king sacrifices for his people. He pitched back his sword. "Come at me, beast."

A shadow burst from shadow; a streak of black rushed toward Pirosha, and Pirosha responded with a swing of his sword. The blade connected and tore across fur, skin, and lean muscle. A bit of blood sprayed Pirosha's mouth, and the dog let out a deafening howl.

The dog pounced on Pirosha, clenched the collar of his shirt in its jaw, and hurled him to the ground hard. Pirosha drew in a shaky gasp as the air left him. Even as he lay there, the dog dug into him with his sharp claws, ripping open the fabric of Pirosha's shirt. It reached toward

Pirosha with its jaw down in an attempt to rip open his throat, but Pirosha—in a burst of strength—hurled the dog off him and stood up, drawing Elvathan as he stumbled forward.

The dog bounded across the square, eyes glowing yellow in the lamplight, huffing in the chill autumn air. Pirosha swung again and his sword connected again, tearing across the dog's hide but only making a shallow cut.

A wail issued from a nearby house. Pirosha looked toward the noise, panting. A norg girl stood at the doorway in a dark dress. Her pale face contorted in fear, and her thin lip trembled. "Don't kill the dog!" she cried. "He's misunderstood!"

"Misunderstood?" Pirosha scoffed. "He's a norg-eater!"

The dog slowly circled him, growling. In the lamplight it became clear to Pirosha that this was a wolfhound, a breed not commonly seen in norgish lands. As he looked into its yellowish eyes, he realized this beast was incredibly large: it stood nearly eye to eye with him.

"Just listen!" the girl screamed again. "Don't hurt him."

But Pirosha ignored her cries and charged the wolfhound, pitching back Elvathan as he ran. The dog pounced, and overcame him, knocking Elvathan out of Pirosha's hand.

Pirosha did his best to hold back the dog's muzzle. This is it. I'm going to die.

Footsteps began, growing louder. Pirosha's body had gone sticky and slick with blood, and he lost more by the second. Then several things happened at once.

A harsh, acrid scent. The sight of powder flung from an unseen hand. The dog yowling and then hitting the floor, unconscious. Pirosha following him into the black.

II.

A face hovered above him, white like the full moon. Dewy chestnut eyes, and pale lips that Pirosha had the urge to kiss. Only after he remembered what went on did he realize that this was the girl from before. The norg girl who tried to stop him from fighting the dog.

Then Pirosha looked down at his body. He wore no shirt, only a cloth covering his groin and legs. Because of that, he could see the huge lacerations running across his chest. They seemed to be healing—the girl knew what she was doing, apparently—but the sight of the deep wounds sent chills up Pirosha's spine.

"What's your name?" Pirosha managed to say.

"Imowyn," the girl replied.

"You're the witch," Pirosha said.

"I'm not a witch. I have no magical talent," Imowyn said. "The people think I'm a witch, because—well—I'm smart, and I know how to make things. I'm like one of the old dwarvish Brewmasters, except with herbs."

"You saved me," Pirosha said. "I owe you thanks."

"You owe me more than that." Imowyn smiled.

Pirosha returned her smile. "What do I owe you? Go ahead."

"We are going to help him."

"Who?"

"The dog!"

Pirosha's smile vanished. "Help that thing? Look at what it did to me!" He gestured to the lacerations.

"I told you! He is misunderstood. His spirit is trapped. A bogey is inside the dog. We need to free the dog's spirit from the bogey so it can go on to the next world…"

Pirosha sighed. "And how would we do that?" He stood up, making sure the cloth around his groin did not fall. His tattered clothes lay in the far corner of the room which—Pirosha noted—was rather small for a dwelling.

"At first I thought we would need common *wolfsbane*, but that won't do," Imowyn said. "We need to go into the Heart of the Sheeh, and we need to find *bloodcup*."

"This dog viciously attacked me, and you expect me to *help* it?"

"It's not him, it's the bogey!"

Bogeys—dark spirits that wreaked havoc on mortals—haunted

shadowy places like the Sheeh. The story, altogether, was not impossible. Just unlikely.

Pirosha spoke firmly. "I will not help a dog that savaged me."

"You owe me."

Her eyes bored into his, innocent and dewy. Her lips trembled. "Fine!" he cried at last.

The Sheeh surrounded the village of Loxdon like a gaping-mouthed monster. Moss draped down from the tightly-clustered trees. Vines wound their way around and across their trunks. In all, the air emanating from the blackness was fragrant, but Pirosha knew the Sheeh had claimed many lives. Some said the Sheeh was an entity of its own and that it hungered for norgs as foolish as Pirosha. He gulped.

Imowyn entered, hugging a bright bull's-eye lantern to her chest. She vanished into the black. After a moment's hesitation, Pirosha entered.

Her lantern provided the only light, and illuminated the trunks of the trees. Occasionally Pirosha saw a face in them. "Where can we find *bloodcup*?" His voice cracked, betraying his fear.

"*Bloodcup* grows on the corpses of dead firvalg."

"Firvalg." Pirosha gulped. Creatures of myth and legend, the half-wolves were said to have disappeared into the Sheeh long ago, and never seen again.

Suddenly the darkness ended, and light blinded Pirosha as they reached a clearing. A bit of rain pattered down as Pirosha looked up at the sky. He smiled. When his eyes adjusted and he looked at the ground, his smile vanished.

A furry creature was stooped over the corpse of some wild animal, smacking as it ate. Specks of blood stained its silver coat. This was a firvalg... or the back of one, at least.

"What will we do?" Pirosha whispered, and then Imowyn looked back at him with bulging eyes and an expression that said, *Are you really that stupid?*

But he had made noise, and the furry creature turned and began to sniff around. Pirosha backed up slowly, drawing against a tree trunk. Imowyn stayed put.

Pirosha could hear the pounding of his heart. *Thud-thud. Thud-thud.*

Then the firvalg dashed away into the darkness of the Sheeh, leaving the mound of torn flesh behind. Imowyn looked back at Pirosha with that same are-you-stupid expression. "You almost got us killed."

Pirosha walked past her through the thick brush and entered the light. The stench of bodily fluids hung heavy in the air.

"Let's go on," Imowyn said.

"Wait."

The corpse was such a mess of flesh and blood that it was hard to discern what it actually was. But it became more and more clear to Pirosha that this was no deer or bear. For one, traces of thick black fur clung to some of the flesh. Also, the head—shredded mess that it was—was clearly lupine. The dead thing was a firvalg. The firvalg had been eating a firvalg.

"Come on!" Imowyn said.

"How long does it take for the *bloodcup* to grow on a newly-dead corpse?"

"Why?"

"This is a firvalg we're looking at."

"A firvalg? Surely not!" Imowyn walked over. "Well... firvalgs are cannibals, and... Oh, dear, you're right!" She and Pirosha exchanged glances. "I have some *bloodcup* seeds in my house, and if they have some flesh to grow in, then they would be ready in a few days. Just cut off an arm—I won't watch!"

She looked away as Pirosha did the deed. Cutting through the thick, sinewy flesh proved much more difficult than Pirosha expected. But at last, after a minute of hacking and sawing and shattering bone, he lifted up the bloody trophy. "You can look now!" he whispered.

As she looked up, the same silver-furred firvalg stepped out of the shadows into the clearing. How strange it was to see something so lupine—with its wet black, whiskery muzzle and piercing blue eyes, and its silver coat of fur—standing on two legs like a norg. It towered above Pirosha, perhaps six feet tall. With the dead firvalg's arm in his hand, Pirosha screamed, "Run!" and he waited until Imowyn had started before he came up behind her at a dead sprint.

The firvalg tore through the brush with its claws, rending the thick clogged growth aside as it bolted forward on its bipedal paws. It let out a piercing howl, and Pirosha's gut clenched.

The light of the outside world appeared through a veil of moss. Another five seconds' sprint, and he would make it; yet his goal seemed impossibly faraway. The musty odor of the firvalg's fur hit his nose, and the beast was close.

A howl resounded from behind. A set of iron jaws clutched the severed firvalg arm, and tore it away from Pirosha, who turned around and saw death in the silverback's blue eyes. The huge firvalg stood up and stretched his arms, puffing out his chest as he howled.

"Come on!" Imowyn said. "There's no use in you dying."

Pirosha turned and ran.

The fresh air hit him, and light was all around him; and he realized he was on the shore of the River Sheogan, and the lights of Loxdon Village lay before him.

"We've failed." Pirosha's eyes moistened.

"I wonder when the firvalg will leave the Sheeh and set our norgish villages to the flame. It's only a matter of time before the spell of binding fades away."

Imowyn just has to make the situation even gloomier, doesn't she? Pirosha sighed. "Let's go rest. We've failed, and failed utterly."

"It's not your fault," Imowyn said, but even she couldn't hide her glum expression. "Let's go rest. You can have my cot, and I'll make nettle tea."

She took the lead. As Pirosha watched from behind, he realized he liked this girl, although he understood why the townsfolk called her a witch. She certainly knew a lot, and her intelligence outmatched Diarsha; the villagers of Loxdon simply did not know how to deal with a girl so smart.

Imowyn barely put her hand round the doorknob of her house when a shout interrupted them.

"Hey! Witch!" Lord Diarsha stood a few yards away near the house opposite. "Look at what we did to your pet!"

The wolfhound lay there, immobile. Its chest heaved with breath, and despite its vulnerable position, a growling was clearly audible.

Imowyn cried out. "You don't understand! You just don't get it!"

She ran up to him, and Pirosha followed. As they neared him, it became apparent that three other villagers stood with Diarsha: three gruff-looking norgish men. One of them held a hatchet.

"You can't just kill everything that's different from you!" Imowyn pleaded.

"Don't tell me what I can and can't do, witch," Diarsha sneered. "You have no right to."

"I do," Pirosha boomed, "and I command you not to harm the dog!"

Diarsha's mouth formed a perfect O. Eventually he laughed and muttered, "What a king you are! One of your subjects asks for help… and you tell them to spare the monster, after allying yourself with a witch."

"She's not a witch," Pirosha said. "A bogey has possessed the dog, and we have the means to cure it."

"We asked for your help, Shortsprout, and we finally had to do it ourselves. Don't get in our way. Toran, land him a solid blow!"

Pirosha moved in to stop him but the hatchet fell hard. Imowyn screamed as it dug into the dog's ribs; and black mist spouted from its body. When the form dissolved, a titan stood in their midst. Twice the size of a Big Person—perhaps ten feet tall—with a thick black beard and dark brown eyes, he was a giant out of myth.

"At last, I am healed!" he said.

"*Kill him*!" Diarsha hissed.

The man with the hatchet ran at him but the giant—still partially obscured by the mist—drew back a large hammer and struck a hard blow. The sledge shattered bone, and the norg went flying across the village square.

"I don't mean to harm you," the giant roared, "but if you run at me again I will kill all of you."

Diarsha ran off, screaming, "To arms! To arms!"

Pirosha stood there in the giant's shadow. "I don't mean any harm to you," he said. "Diarsha is small and petty. I am King of Kalamar."

"Pretty short for a king, aren't you?" the giant rumbled.

"He may be short," Imowyn said, "but he is kind, and brave, and most of all he is a good listener."

Pirosha blushed.

"Aye," the giant said. "I suppose size isn't everything."

"What is your name?" Imowyn asked. "And where do you come from?"

"I am Donner Redshield, and I come from far away. I wandered into this strange country here—this tangle of vines and brush…"

"The Sheeh," Pirosha explained.

"Aye. And the last thing I remember before I turned into a dog is two yellow eyes in the darkness."

"A bogey!" Imowyn cried in elation. "I was right!"

Pirosha smiled. "You seem to be right very often, Imowyn."

Imowyn giggled. "Thanks."

"Will you come with me to the Dain? Your skills as an herbalist would really help," Pirosha said.

"I've never been to the capital province," Imowyn said. "My parents are dead, and I have no friends here… so yes, I will come with you. I must only pack my things."

"In elder times, before my imprisonment, I served Lord Bayne, king of Kalamar," Donner thundered, "so I will pledge service to you as well, my king."

"You knew Lord Bayne? The ancestor of the norgs?" Pirosha asked incredulously.

Donner nodded. "Aye, and Bayne's people had beards, unlike you; and they wore fine steel armor, and their buildings were of stone, not this wood and hay."

"It will be my honor to have you in the Dain," Pirosha said.

Imowyn gathered her things, stuffing several bags worth of books and many more bags worth of herbs and vials. At last, she gathered her donkey from the communal stables (located in the inn) and loaded the poor beast with all her baggage. Then they left.

But waiting there on the bridge over the River Sheogan was Lord Diarsha. Behind him were the three norgs from before, plus a few others. This time, all of them bore axes.

"We declare our secession from the Kingdom of Kalamar," Diarsha said. "I am now King of Loxdon and I will hear of nothing else."

Pirosha drew his sword. *How dare he?* "You will acknowledge my kingship, Diarsha, or you will lose your sovereignty over Loxdon."

"I will not budge," Diarsha said. "I will not let you over the river unless you call me king."

Pirosha clenched his teeth and he began to shake. "Why, you…"

"Milord," Donner bellowed, "If I may—"

"Go ahead."

Donner walked up to the bridge with thunderous steps. The wooden bridge groaned under his weight as Diarsha's five soldiers looked up with wide eyes and trembling bodies. He pitched back his hammer and they scrambled away. Only Lord Diarsha remained.

"I will not budge for you, brute!"

Donner picked Diarsha up by the leg, shook him as he screamed, and finally, tossed the lord into the water.

Pirosha cheered for Donner and Imowyn followed.

As the River Sheogan carried Lord Diarsha away, Pirosha let out a hearty laugh and then, the three companions walked across the bridge toward the Dain as the sun arose in glimmering gold over the eastern sky.

Next, read the first chapter of Nocturne, Son of the Night.

CHAPTER ONE
NO JOY IN BLOOD

Monsters—that's what outsiders call us. Human or otherwise, they never come to our lands; they only murmur in dim-lit taverns, telling horror stories over glasses of ale. They turn my race, the Druen, into bloodsucking murderers, and their skills at fabrication know no limit. But despite this, I like to think my heart, though it does not beat, is far from dead.

I grew up in a fishing village on the coast. Drastheon is small, but I've always been proud of my town. We do not practice the dark rites of the capital, where the soldiers sacrifice every firstborn child as a bloodmeal to the rich.

Of course, if we did practice that rite, my family would benefit. As a member of the House Rabaam, I resided in the largest home in Drastheon. Our home, simply called "The Manor," was sprawling and huge, composed of stone, with a red tile roof. It lay toward the outskirts of town. The out-of-town royals and bards often remarked favorably about Manor's innards. We had only the finest furnishings: glass cups, painted porcelain dishes, varnished teak furniture, and ornamental eggs. Despite this, we tried to withhold our pretensions; some of the less fortunate in Drastheon despised us for our luck. But it really wasn't luck, you see.

My grandfather was responsible for it all. My parents named me after him: Dralynthi. Nocturne. He was a well-known entrepreneur. His business consisted of the purchase and sale of slaves—mostly Elven slaves, but sometimes humans picked from the far reaches. They would cook, or clean, or sleep with their masters, but their lives always ended as a blood meals, when they grew old or ineffectual. This had been the fate of all our family slaves—Men and Elves, girls and boys.

I was twenty years old, one unseasonably cold day in what should have been late spring. A deep layer of snow covered the roofs of the houses and huts.

A cluster of ramshackle buildings surrounded the village square. In the center was a stand where I could always find the fishmonger. He sold haddock, fresh blue haddock, every day. He sold his produce every day, without fail, except for feast-days. He'd been in the trade since before I was born.

Right beside him, just a few yards away, I noticed something different: a wooden cage. It was composed of varnished pinewood bars. Yet the thing inside was the most interesting part. A human stood there. She was about my age. She looked young, and her skin was smooth and un-blistered by work. Her hair, a dark brown, hung to her hips in a long ponytail. Her thin, dark brows complemented her deep blue eyes perfectly. And yet her demeanor struck me, most of all.

Most slaves shook and cried and begged for freedom, when they came to Druen lands. They never earned our sympathy.

Yet this girl was not afraid. She had a look that seemed to say, "Try me."

As my gaze upon her lingered, my reaction surprised me. A deep desire overcame me. She was the most beautiful creature I'd ever seen. I knew very little of her, truly, but I imagined everything else: strong and un-submissive, but with a good heart behind the iron shell.

Humans were off limits as wives. Having any meaningful relationship with her would brand me as a traitor to my pure Elvish race. This aversion to human relations was common among all the Elf Tribes—but with the Druen, doing so carried the penalty of death. Yet looking at this girl—this slave—did more things to me than any person I had ever met in Drastheon or elsewhere.

"Nocturne!" shouted a voice I knew very well. The voice of my neighbor, Dreddani. The salutation was accompanied, as I expected, by a pungent wave of body odor.

I suppressed a groan. "Dreddani," I said.

"Cold day, eh?"

"Yes."

"Strange weather for this late in the year, eh?"

"Yes."

"Snow's sure pilin' up, eh?"

I said nothing. Neither did he, for a while. I thanked every god and spirit whenever Dreddani's mouth was shut. Such rare occasions were a divine gift. I say this only as a matter of speech; I do not believe in the gods, or that anything should be called a god.

Dreddani spoke again; proof for my disbelief. "Pretty good lookin' slave they got there. She'd make a good maid. O' course, she might very well do more than cleanin', eh? Eh?"

I sighed.

"I got three crowns saved up. I might buy her, maybe, if no one wants her."

"You're too poor to outbid me," I said.

"You want her?" Dreddani put one of his meaty hands on my shoulder.

I flinched. "Not necessarily."

"Well, then I might buy her. I might bed her and then drink 'er dry."

I shook his hand off my shoulder and snarled. "That is an incredible waste, Dreddani! A complete waste of a healthy slave. Three crowns for one night of fun, and a good dinner—doesn't that sound impulsive? And incredibly idiotic?"

"Well, I don't know."

I struck him hard with my hand and he yelped. I headed back home. And completely forgot about dinner.

My mother, Drassané, threw a fit when she saw my empty hands. "Nocturne Gangimmi Emorthi Drethuli Rabaam!"

I had long learned to block out her shrill voice. She was old and old-fashioned, in her late 160s. She wore a necklace of pearls and paid excessive attention to her graying hair.

My father was similarly old and old-fashioned, in his early 200s, and had a very antiquated view on life: Marry only a Druen from your home village; lie with one woman, your wife; do not drink the blood of your fellow Druen. Control your bloodlust and only drink when you must, and when it is appropriate and civil.

"You must march right back and get us our dinner," Mother said, and sighed. "Oh, Nocturne, you're so scatterbrained."

I nodded. "Yes, mother." I turned and opened the door a crack.

"I love you, Nocturne."

"I love you too, Mother."

The fishmonger's produce was crusted over by ice. Only eight fish remained. The slave girl stood a few yards away, her hands grasping the bars.

I approached the fishmonger briskly. "I'll have some haddock."

Scars covered every inch of the fisherman's face. He always had the appearance of biting into a sour grape. "Four for two silver," he said. "By the way, this girl's three crowns. Nice deal, if I do say so myself."

"You're selling her?" I asked.

"Yeh. Came by this morning," said the fishmonger. "Three crowns, that's it."

I trudged up to the girl. I was a little nervous. "What's your name?" I said.

Her eyes narrowed. She frowned. "My name is 'Shut-Your-Fangs.'"

I smiled faintly. She had boundless energy, something good for a wife. But this marriage would have to be secret.

"What's your name, really?" I asked.

"Go away," she said.

I walked over and tossed two silver coins onto the fishmonger's table. Then I walked back to the cage and said, "I'm Nocturne." I reached through the cage bars and forced her to look at me. I said, "You are pretty."

"Don't make me hit you," she said, eyeing my groin.

I ran my fingers along her cheek. "You are so tense," I said.

She jerked away. "I'll scream, if you touch me again."

"What good would that do?"

The fishmonger called out, "Nocturne! You gonna take your haddock, or you gonna sit there 'n flirt? Come on!"

He successfully redirected my attention. I grabbed a handful of the frozen haddock. Hopefully, Mother would make a good dinner tonight.

Mother served the pan-fried haddock on silver plates. It was delicious. But my thoughts drifted constantly, back to the slave and how cheaply I could free her. And how no one had ever drawn me in so strongly. What did I have to lose? I had everything to gain.

She was rude, but perhaps if she got to know me, she would like me more. By the time I had placed the last bit of haddock in my mouth, and drank the last drop of mead from my cup, I had made my decision.

I would march straight back to the village square and purchase her for the three crowns she was going for.

Yet when I returned, she was gone. The fishmonger was packing up his wooden table, apparently ready to go home.

"What happened to the girl?" I asked. I clutched the three gold coins in my fingers, feeling like a fool.

"Oh, her?" he asked. "Eh, Dreddani bought 'er. You're too late."

"Dreddani!" The fat bastard would probably do what he said he would—lie with her and drink her dry. She deserved more than that fat pig, even if she was human. She deserved an upstanding Druen from a good family, someone who thought more of her than as a bloodmeal. She deserved me.

I dashed down the road, as fast as I could. Snowflakes drifted from the sky with blinding number, and a freezing wind blasted out of the sea. I ran down the road, knowing that I had very little time. It took only a minute or so to fully drink a human's blood. I sprinted as hard as I could, but my legs just wouldn't carry me any faster.

I passed by the Manor, where my mother and father were doubtlessly reclining, unaware of the slave-girl's plight. Dreddani's house was a short run from there. I continued my sprint, knowing I'd soon collapse in exhaustion; I wasn't used to running. Finally, I arrived.

Someone screamed from inside Dreddani's shack. I dashed at the door, blood boiling in my veins. My fangs contracted of their own accord. I dashed to his doorstep and gave it a powerful kick, but it wouldn't budge. I kicked it again and again. With each kick the door splintered; the hinges shuddered and weakened.

Dreddani's voice called out from within. "Who the hell is it?"

"Help me!" screamed the slave-girl.

I kicked harder than ever and the door gave way, splitting open with a loud crack. Dreddani had his fangs sunk into the girl's neck, drinking her down fast. My mind burned, my hands shook, with anger.

I charged at him, and ripped him away. Two puncture-holes pocked the slave-girl's neck.

I sank my fangs into his neck. Felt his blood rush up through my gums. The high was indescribable. The arousing blood took my mind soaring to unthinkable heights. I drank deeply, as Dreddani struggled against me. For a second, I thought I could understand the passion of the Morthen, who dedicated their life to pursuing the Druen's greatest pleasure.

I continued until Dreddani weakened. He was fat and out of shape, and soon his legs gave out. And yet, once I had drunk the last drop of blood, I questioned the immense pleasure. The unfulfilling sensation seemed so pointless. Regret overcame me and I realized there is no joy in blood.

The girl was ashen-faced. She had fallen onto the floor, her body gone limp. I would rescue her. I would take care of her. I grabbed her and lifted her into my arms, letting her head recline on my shoulder.

I staggered outside into the blinding snow. It seemed like the darkest depths of winter had come once again, with its endless nights and penetrating cold. Down the road, I saw a village boy running towards town screaming about my betrayal. Soon, the whole village be roused. I was a traitor; I had murdered a Druen for the sake of a slave.

I dashed through the doors of the Manor with the slave in my arms. I frantically told my mother what happened, as I held the slave's unconscious body.

The tears started pouring. "Oh, Nocturne, you fool! You damnable fool! They'll kill you, you know. You damned foolish boy." She sobbed. "Oh, they'll kill you now. Why in the world would you do this? Run, Nocturne. And don't forget me."

"I could never forget you, Mother."

I set her down briefly and ran for the closet. I grabbed a large bearskin coat and wrapped the slave-girl within it. Humans, unlike Druen, can die from cold weather. I went to the kitchen, and grabbed a satchel full of dried fish.

Then, I left.

The town sounded the alarm. They grabbed daggers and knives and fishing-spears; whatever they could kill me with. They ran out of their homes to look for me, but I slipped into the taiga. I ran into the forest eaves with Katrina in my arms.

I had betrayed my race for a human girl. As I dashed into the icy pine forest, I knew what I had done. I had sacrificed my life on a whim. I had ruined any chance of living in Drastheon.

I had made the right decision.

www.ingramcontent.com/pod-product-compliance
Lightning Source LLC
Chambersburg PA
CBHW020612250626
47154CB00004B/1477